CASH

SILVER SAINTS MC

FIONA DAVENPORT

CASH

SILVER SAINTS MC

Cassius "Cash" Gannon wasn't thrilled to be assigned babysitting duty that required him to head all the way to Aspen to pick up his charge. But then he met Karina Timkins, and he realized she was the light that he needed in his life.

Determined to do whatever it took to keep Karina safe from the mess her father had created, he brought her back to the Silver Saints compound. Where she found the family she'd always wanted.

1

KARINA

"I can't believe we're really going to spend Christmas in Aspen with Dad." I hummed in pleasure as I took a sip of my hot chocolate. "And in such an awesome cabin with a fireplace in practically every room."

Curled up on the opposite side of the couch, my mom beamed a soft smile at me. "You know how much he loves his creature comforts."

I'd taken plenty of vacations during my eighteen years, but this was the first over Christmas. We usually stuck close to home during the holidays since my dad's travel schedule for work was so hectic. It wasn't unusual for him to be called away after dinner on Christmas Eve or not to make it home until after my mom and I had already had breakfast on the big day.

His clients were demanding, but he always told me that was why they paid him the big bucks. Not that his explanation helped soothe the pain of missing him when he was gone. But I refused to think about all the holidays he'd missed when he would be joining us in a few days for Christmas.

"Well, he's outdone himself this time."

My mom raised her mug toward me, her smile widening. "Of course, he did. We only get one chance to celebrate your graduation from high school. And since you finished a semester early, this trip is even more special because we're spending the holiday together as a family in such a beautiful place."

"Yeah, I wasn't too sure about Aspen when Dad suggested it since skiing isn't exactly my idea of fun, but the view is gorgeous, and there's other stuff to do like ice skating and sledding."

My mom nudged my e-reader toward me with her foot. "And reading in front of the fireplace."

"Definitely," I agreed.

Writing, too. But my mom didn't know that my journaling had transitioned to fictional stories in recent months. I wasn't ready to share that secret with anyone yet. Not until I finished the story I was working on. Maybe not even then since I didn't want to hurt her, which was bound to happen since the heroine of my mystery novel had serious daddy issues. And there was no denying that they'd been inspired by my own.

Almost as though my dad could hear me thinking about him halfway across the country, my mom's phone rang. I knew it was him calling because he was the only person who'd ever filled her eyes with the particular mix of passion and love shining from them as she tapped her finger against the screen. "Happy Christmas Eve Eve! Besides wishing you were here already, you'll never guess what Karina and I are doing right now."

"I need you to take me off speaker, Stephanie."

My mom's eyes widened at my dad's tone, and stark disappointment crashed over me. I'd never heard him sound like that, and I figured he didn't want me to hear his excuses for canceling on us when he knew how special this trip was to me. My shoulders slumped while my mom did as he demanded, but I stayed where I was instead of heading into the bedroom my best friend and I had claimed when we arrived yesterday. Between the ski lesson she'd had yesterday morning and jet lag, Lorelei was exhausted. I didn't want to disturb her nap even though I had a strong feeling I would need one of her comforting hugs soon.

A few minutes later, my prediction came true. Just for a reason much worse than I expected.

My mom's cheeks were pale as she switched back to speaker mode. Her voice shook as she said, "Karina, honey. Your father needs to tell you something."

"Let me guess...you're not coming?" I whispered.

"Sorry, sweetheart, but being close to me isn't safe for you right now."

My head jerked back. "What? Why?"

"I...shit, I don't know how to tell you this even though I've already done it once."

"Done what once?" I echoed, my brows drawing together as I tried to guess what could be happening. The way he sounded, my mom's reaction, him swearing when he rarely did...meant something big was happening. "Just tell me."

"Someone wants to use you to hurt me."

I twisted to the left and stretched out my arm to set my hot chocolate on the end table, my stomach turning at the thought of taking another sip. "A client? Or someone who isn't happy that you're a better lawyer than the one they hired?"

"No, sweetheart. A man who offered me money to make sure his son remained free after doing the unthinkable."

I felt as though I had entered an alternate universe as my dad explained that he'd gotten involved in a judicial bribery scheme and how a ruthless man wanted revenge against him after he hadn't held up his end of the bargain. The man's son had received a death sentence when my dad had been unable to intervene after he'd been removed from the bench, and the guy apparently thought the only fitting way to make my dad pay was through me. A daughter's life in exchange for a son's.

So many things were wrong with what he'd told me that it was hard to know where to begin. "I don't understand. How can you be a judge and a lawyer at the same time?"

"I'm not. I took a seat on the bench five years ago."

My mom's hands trembled too much for her to hold the phone, so she set it on the cushion between us before she asked, "You've been lying to us this whole time?"

"I'm sorry." He heaved a deep sigh. "For much longer than that."

My mom couldn't have been aware of anything he was telling us. She looked as shocked as I felt. "What did you mean when you said you've already done this once?"

"He went after Kiara first, but a local motorcycle club, the Silver Saints, got involved and they were able to negotiate a deal with him to protect her. If I'd had any idea that Bickle knew about you, I swear I would have let them know sooner. They never would have agreed to his deal to leave her alone if they'd known he'd go after my other daughter."

"Kiara? You have another daughter?" my mom gasped.

I moved closer to her and wrapped my arms around her shoulders. Her whole body was shaking as tears streamed down her cheeks, but she was silent as she cried.

"I have a sister?" I whispered, biting my lip to hold back my tears.

"Yes, she's a year older than you and just finished her first semester of college."

I'd always wondered why they'd never gotten married after being together for so long. But my mom had never seemed bothered by it, so I'd stopped asking questions about it years ago. Now I wished I had kept pushing. Maybe if I had, his secrets would have come out sooner.

Pressing her knuckles against her lips, she mumbled, "Her mom?"

My dad's voice cracked as he answered, "She's my wife, but I swear to you that we haven't lived as a married couple since you came into my life all those years ago."

"Then why is she still your wife?" I hissed.

"Because I couldn't leave Kiara behind with her, and that was the only way she was ever going to let me out of our marriage. Marsha doesn't care about anything except appearances, not even our daughter. And by the time Kiara turned eighteen, it was too late for me to get out because I was already wrapped up in this damn mess. I couldn't afford to have my life ripped into without exposing what I'd gotten myself into. But as soon as my house of cards started falling apart—before Bickle threatened Kiara—I talked to a divorce lawyer."

Mom sagged against the back of the couch at his confession. "I guess that's something, at least."

"I'm sorry, Stephanie. I never wanted you to find out this way," he apologized.

"Over the phone? Before you were divorced? Or

after you had to tell me that you've put our daughter's life in danger?" she snarled.

"I'm so fucking sorry I'm not there to hold you while you cry. I'd be there in a heartbeat if it wouldn't make it easier for Bickle to find Karina. Even with the Silver Saints already headed your way, it's too dangerous for me to be near her until they've tracked him down again."

All I could do was hold my mom as her shoulders shook while she cried, "I shouldn't ever want to see you again, but I can't help wishing you were here."

"Who are the Silver Saints?" I asked.

"They're the ones who figured out what I was doing when I..." He paused and muttered, "Shit," then sighed again before continuing. "I was going to imprison one of their men for a crime he didn't commit."

I didn't even want to ask how he'd gotten them to help after what he'd done to one of the members. I couldn't take another revelation about him today. Or anytime soon, most likely. He'd already destroyed everything I'd ever thought about him.

"And Mom's not at risk?"

"No, he's only interested in hurting my daughters, and he's given up on going after Kiara because he knows the Silver Saints will never stop hunting him if he does anything to her. So that only leaves you."

"As hurt as I am by all of this, you have a lot more explaining to do to Mom. You've betrayed her more than me." I swallowed the lump in my throat.

"I know." He sounded genuinely broken, and it tugged at my heartstrings, but I was madder than I'd ever been, and I shoved those feelings away.

"You have protection for Karina?" my mom asked quietly, her tone strained.

"Yes. They're on their way there now."

"I don't want anything from you," I insisted, my voice shaking with anger. "I can take care of myself."

"Please, Karina?" My mom took my hands and met my gaze with pleading eyes. "I need to know you are safe, and your dad and I need to talk about this face-to-face. I can't leave you unprotected."

"Fine," I muttered. They better be prepared to protect me here for the full length of the reservation because I had no intention of leaving with strangers to go who the heck knew where. I did want them to answer some questions for me, though.

The relief in his voice was impossible to miss, but it didn't soften the anger I was feeling. "I'm not doing this for you."

"I know, but I'll take it just the same because your safety means the world to me."

I nearly snorted in derision at that, except deep down, I still loved my dad and wanted to know that despite everything, he loved me.

My dad offered to arrange everything for my mom's flight, then we hung up, and I focused on what Mom needed to do to get ready to go to the airport. That included urging Lorelei to hit the slopes when she woke up from her nap because I couldn't handle her questions about what was happening. I refused to think about my dad or what he'd confessed to doing. Or the danger I was in. My dad called back once he'd worked out my mom's flight details. He also told me that the guys the Silver Saints had sent to protect me had already landed in Aspen and would be here soon. Not that I had any intention of letting them take over my life when there were no signs that the guy who wanted me dead had any idea I was in Aspen.

However, I was curious to know why these guys were willing to protect me after what my dad did. And my dad had mentioned that they were protecting...my...my sister—that felt so weird to think—and I was confused as to why they were willing to risk their necks for us.

When my dad had called the second time, I'd tried to ask him about it, but he would only tell me that we'd talk about it later. Well, if he wouldn't do it, then I would get these Silver Saints guys to answer my queries.

After dropping off my mom, I returned to the cabin and found a note from Lorelei. She'd taken me up on my suggestion and gone to the slopes. I'd told her that something had come up with my dad and my mom had to fly back without going into any details, so she was oblivious to the drama unfolding. At least for now.

I glanced around, and the idea of leaving this beautiful place where I was supposed to have spent the perfect holiday broke something inside me. It was yet another thing my dad's secrets had stolen from me.

I sat and stared at the fire until there was a knock on the door. Swinging it open, I found two men on the snowy doorstep...at least until the one closest to me shoved the second into a snowdrift. I couldn't seem to tear my eyes away from him to check if the other guy was okay. He was more than a full foot taller than me, with thick, dark hair, a short-trimmed beard and mustache, deep brown eyes, and enough muscles that his winter clothing couldn't hide them.

And I had to wonder if I was more broken by what had happened than I realized because I wanted to throw myself into his arms so he could make it all better.

"I hate the fucking cold," I grumbled as Grey and I stomped up to the cabin door and shook the snow off our boots. I'd grown up in Arizona and lived my whole life in the heat. There was a chill in my fucking bones, but it was nothing compared to the fury burning inside me. Since when was I a fucking babysitter? We had prospects for this shit.

But Mac, the president of the Silver Saints MC, had given me the order. And I couldn't exactly blame Knight for wanting to send a brother to retrieve his old lady's sister. But that didn't mean I had to be happy about it. I'd traipsed my ass all the way up to Aspen because the stubborn little brat refused to come to us for protection.

When we were standing at the door to the big,

fancy ski cabin (which was probably paid for by dirty money), I raised my fist and pounded it against the wood.

Grey sighed and reached across my front to press the doorbell. "Gonna scare her off if you don't stop acting like a hungry grizzly."

Before I could spit out my scathing response, the door opened, and my entire world tilted on its axis.

"Damn," Grey breathed. "Oomph! Shit!"

My hand involuntarily shot out and shoved him off the porch into a large snowdrift. I didn't bother to look his way or check to make sure he wasn't hurt. All of my attention was on the goddess standing before me. Warmth flowed through my veins like I'd just stepped into the hot sun.

She was tiny—no more than five feet tall. At six foot four, I towered over her, and it made me want to scoop her up into my arms and carry her around. Feelings of possession welled up inside me, along with my protective instincts.

The woman in front of me had to be Karina. She resembled her sister, Kiara, but this girl was even more stunning. She looked up at me with big deep-blue eyes, and her high cheekbones had a dusting of pink. Her rosebud mouth inspired fantasies of those lips wrapped around my cock.

Her long golden-blond hair was piled on top of her head, showing off her slender neck and plump cleavage because she was wearing a sweater that fell casually off one shoulder. That drew my eyes to a spectacular pair of tits that should have seemed too big for her frame but somehow looked natural with the rest of her alluring curves. Her body was thick and sexy as hell. Perfect for fucking hard and having babies.

What the fuck? I had no idea where that thought had come from, but once it was there, my cock—which had jumped to attention the second I saw her—turned rock hard and pressed against my jeans like it was trying to break free to reach my girl's pussy. I was fully on board with that but knew it wasn't the time to act on those instincts.

"Hi," she said softly, her lips curving into a flirty smile.

"Hey," I responded, my tone gruffer than I'd intended. I struggled to control the lust threatening to consume me.

Her expression faltered, and I felt guilty for being such an asshole. However, what happened next wasn't going to improve her opinion of me, which only increased my irritation.

"You Karina?"

She cocked her head to the side and studied me with an expression that had turned wary. "Yes."

"Cash." I tilted my head toward Grey. "Grey."

Her brow furrowed a little, and my fingers itched to smooth it out, which shocked me because it seemed like something a mushy sap would do.

I shook the impulse off and said, "We're Silver Saints."

Karina's whole body stiffened, and anger took over her features. The fire in her eyes was hot as hell, and for the first time, I was grateful for the cold because it kept my erection from getting out of control and scaring the shit out of her.

"I'm not going with you," she snapped.

I forced back a grin at her display of fire. "It's cold as fuck out here, sunshine. How about we talk inside?"

"We can talk here," she insisted, raising her chin to a stubborn angle.

She wasn't able to hide her shivers, though, so I grabbed her around the waist, ignoring her gasp, and lifted her out of our way so we could walk into the cabin.

She huffed and slammed the door, clearly annoyed. Then she marched past me into a large, open space with three comfy-looking couches, blankets and pillows strewed about. A big stone fireplace glowed from the ashes of a recent flame.

Karina flopped onto one of the couches and crossed her arms under her tits, emphasizing the generous globes. I had to fight not to let her perfect breasts captivate my attention. "Fine."

I ambled to where she'd taken a seat and lowered myself down less than a foot away from her. "How long will it take you to pack up?" I asked.

Her eyes narrowed, and she shook her head. "I'm not going anywhere until I get some questions answered."

I admired her straightforward attitude and wanted to tell her anything she asked. But Mac had been clear that I should get in and get out as quickly as possible. And I wasn't sure just how much the prez would share with her. "I promise, you'll get your questions answered when we get home." *Some of them.*

"Why not now?"

"Because we need to grab your shit and get you to safety as fast as possible." I expected her to jump up and run to get her stuff, but she didn't move a muscle.

"Do you know my sister?"

"Yes." That wasn't revealing much.

"Why are you guys protecting her?"

"That conversation can wait," I sighed. I would leave that up to Knight and Kiara. Karina deserved to learn about her sister directly from the source. "Go get your shit together so we can get out of here."

"I want answers now," she argued, unfolding her arms and jumping to her feet. "And I'm not going anywhere until I get some!"

I stood, straightening to my full height so I towered over her. My voice was hard and unyielding when I responded. "That wasn't a request, Karina."

We stared each other down for several minutes until she finally threw her hands in the air and exclaimed in frustration. Then she spun on her heel and stomped across the living space and into a bedroom, then slammed the door shut behind her. I grunted in annoyance when I heard the click of the lock.

I'd be able to pick it in seconds, throw her over my shoulder, and get the hell out of Dodge. But I sensed that I needed to tread carefully so I didn't scare her away or drive a wedge between us before I even had the chance to draw her in.

"Damn." I swiveled my head to see Grey lounging on one of the other sofas, staring at the door my girl had just disappeared through. "She's got some fire."

"Mine," I snapped.

Grey raised an eyebrow, but he didn't look surprised. "I figured."

Just then, the knob on the front door jiggled, and Grey and I were over there, guns drawn, in seconds. When it swung open, there was a girl with skis and a bright smile that died the moment she spotted the weapons in our hands.

"Who are you?" she screeched, dropping her equipment and rushing inside. "Where's Karina? What have you done? I'm calling the police!"

Before I could form a thought and answer her, Grey stalked over and wrapped his hands around her waist before practically tossing the girl over his shoulder. "I'll take care of this," he growled as he turned to leave the cabin.

The girl was kicking out and yelling at him to put her down, but he ignored her and slammed the front door behind him.

I was tempted to do the same with Karina, and I even marched over to the bedroom she'd locked herself in. But when I heard her crying, something squeezed my heart, and I decided to give her the night to come around. If she still refused to leave the following morning, I'd go the kidnapping route.

Rather than finding another bedroom to crash in, I stretched out onto one of the long, overstuffed couches. I wanted Karina's room in my sight. Partly so I could protect her but also because I wanted to make sure she didn't sneak out. Although, even if she did, I would track her ass down. She belonged to me.

3

KARINA

It was good that I'd slept so well the two nights
we'd been in Aspen because I barely got a wink
after those guys from the Silver Saints showed up.
Locked in my bedroom, I couldn't stop thinking
about how my whole world had shifted on its axis. At
first, I stewed over my reaction to the sexy biker my
dad had sent to protect me. Then I brooded about all
the awful secrets he'd finally exposed to my mom
and me.

Finally, in the middle of the night, I realized that
I hadn't thought about the fact that Lorelei had never
returned from skiing. I felt like the world's worst best
friend, even after I found a text from her number
letting me know that she was okay but had a million

questions about what the heck was going on and why a sexy biker of her own had practically kidnaped her.

Rolling over with a soft sigh, I wrapped my arms around a pillow as I stared at the door I'd slammed shut and locked after running from Cash.

Almost as though he could see through the wood surface or somehow managed to hear me, Cash called, "C'mon, sunshine. Don't make me break the door down to get to you."

Climbing off the mattress, I padded across the room to sit down on the floor, leaning my back against the door. "Only if you promise you won't take me back right away. I want to wake up on Christmas morning here, even if it's without my parents."

"I'm not in the habit of making promises I can't keep, and I already told my prez that I'd bring you back to the compound so we can keep you safe."

I appreciated that he was being honest with me... and that keeping his word seemed important to him. After learning that my dad wasn't the man that I'd always thought him to be, I had a feeling that trust would never come easily to me again. "It's Christmas Eve. I bet he's got all sorts of plans. He probably wouldn't even notice if we waited a few days before leaving."

"That's not the way the Silver Saints roll,

sunshine. Mac is not gonna forget that I'm supposed to come back with you just because it's Christmas tomorrow."

There was a trace of regret as he shot down my suggestion, and it gave me hope that I could figure out a way to get Cash to agree to stay. I just needed to be smart about it and come up with a solution that worked for him. "What if your president said it was okay for us to stay longer?"

"Only way that'll happen is if he knows Bickle isn't gonna come here to try to get his hands on you."

My back straightened, and I twisted to stare at the door we were talking through. "Is there any way to track him?"

"Mac has had guys on his trail ever since your dad came clean about you to Kiara."

Although they hadn't been looking for him that long, I asked, "Could you call your president to see if they're any closer to finding him?"

"I don't get why you're being so damn stubborn about this. I would've thought that you had long enough to come to terms with heading to the Silver Saints compound. "

"Long enough? Are you freaking kidding me?" Ruled by the fury coursing through my veins, I jumped to my feet and yanked the door open to glare at Cash. "It's only been half a day since my entire world fell apart."

"Half a day?" he echoed, his brows drawing together.

I nodded, crossing my arms against my chest. "Yeah, my dad called three, maybe four hours before you guys showed up."

"Shit," he grunted, raking his fingers through his dark hair. "He knew when my flight landed and couldn't put it off any longer. Waited until the last possible moment, like a fucking coward, instead of giving you the extra day you would've had while I was making the arrangements needed to get to you without leading Bickle straight to you."

My lips parted, but I pressed them together. My dad didn't deserve to have me defend him, and now I had something else to be angry with him about. My shoulders slumped as I whispered, "I really could've used that extra time to wrap my head around all the crap he told me he's done."

"Fuck, sunshine." Cash wrapped his arms around my back and pulled me against his strong body. "I hate seeing you so upset."

Burying my face against his broad chest, I cried for what felt like hours. I wasn't sure how I even had any tears left in my body since I'd done a ton of crying throughout the night, but I couldn't seem to stop.

When I finally pulled myself together, I tilted my head back to stare up at Cash. "Thank you."

"I'll call Mac and see if they have any leads on where Bickle might be bunkered down. If he thinks you'll be safe here for a little longer, I'll ask if we can stay," he offered.

Pressing my hands together, I gasped, "Yes, please."

"Go wash your face, sunshine." He nudged me back into the bedroom before pulling his cell phone from the back pocket of his jeans and striding away.

I wanted to know what his president would say, but I didn't want to risk pushing Cash when he'd just made a major concession. So I padded over to the bathroom and cleaned up before changing into a new outfit—one that just so happened to look really good on me.

When I headed to the living room, Cash was just finishing his call. His dark eyes scanned my face before they met mine, and I held my breath as I waited for the verdict. "Although we don't currently have his location, there's no indication that Bickle has tracked you here. We've laid a false trail for him leading to Miami, so we should be safe here for a little while."

"Past Christmas?" I croaked.

He paused before answering, "Yes."

The tears that filled my eyes this time were from relief and happiness. "Thank you."

"Don't thank me yet," he warned. "You're gonna need to follow a few rules while we're here."

"What are they?" I asked, even though I felt desperate enough to agree to just about anything.

"No exploring the ski resort, we stay in the cabin, and I'm the only one who answers the door when we order food."

That made sense, so it was easy to agree. "Sure."

"If the situation changes and we need to get outta here, you do as I say so I can keep you safe."

"Okay, I can do that," I murmured, hoping like heck that never happened.

"And you're on an information blackout. No cell phone. No questions. Not until we're back in Silver Saints territory."

My eyes widened as I shook my head. "But I—"

He held his hand up, a muscle jumping in his jaw. "If you can't do it, then we'll have to leave now, even if I have to take you the hard way."

I had so many questions about why the Silver

Saints were helping my dad protect me...and the half sister I'd never known about. But I had to balance my need for answers against the urgent desire I felt to stay in this cabin for as long as I could. To remain in the safety of this bubble before I had to face the reality of what my dad had done. To spend the holiday in front of the gorgeous fireplace in the living room like I'd planned from the moment I saw it, even if my parents weren't with me. "I guess I can keep my questions to myself for now. Except for one... what about Lorelei?"

An odd gleam in his eyes shone as he murmured, "You don't need to worry. Grey has her covered."

Planting my hand on my hip, I glared up at him. "Are you sure she's safe with him? The text she sent me said he basically kidnapped her when she came back from skiing."

His deep chuckle sent a delicious shiver down my spine. "Grey will do whatever it takes to ensure nobody lays a finger on her as long as he's by her side."

I was relieved that my best friend had someone watching her back since I felt awful for pulling her into my dad's mess. And ruining her holiday, along with mine.

CASH SURPRISED me over the next two days, giving me room to come to terms with the things my dad had done while taking care of me. He made sure I ate, didn't complain about the endless stream of holiday movies I zoned out to in the living room, and made the best hot chocolate I'd ever tasted. With marshmallows and whipped cream.

He was the only person I saw or spoke to since he'd arrived, and I was relieved that he didn't seem to mind that I wasn't up to talking about anything other than the snowy weather, food, and movies. I was content in our little bubble, so it came as a shock when he faced off with me in the kitchen when we finished our breakfast the morning after Christmas.

"We're leaving today, sunshine."

My brows drew together as I asked, "Is that guy on his way here?"

"There's been no sign that he's tracked you here yet, but we can't stay here forever. I need to get you to the compound, where there's zero chance of Bickle getting his hands on you."

If we didn't need to leave for safety reasons, then I wasn't going to make this easy on him. Leaning back in my seat, I crossed my arms and shook my head. "No, I'm not ready yet."

Getting to his feet, Cash circled the small table and leaned over me, pressing his hands against the table and back of my chair to cage me in. "I get that being here for Christmas was important to you. I gave you that, but now you've had more time to come to terms with what's happening. Staying a couple more days isn't gonna help you understand. We're leaving today."

I learned that he meant what he said when he tossed me over his shoulder after hauling my stuff to his rental truck.

4

CASH

Karina was still fuming when we drove through the gate and parked near the front door. She'd stewed all the way to the airport, on the plane, and the drive home. I was a little surprised she hadn't blown up yet. All that repressed emotion would need to be released eventually. I knew the perfect way for her to work out all that aggression, but she wasn't ready for me to strip her bare and fuck her until she couldn't move.

She hopped out of the truck and put her hands on her hips, glancing all around her. I opened the back door on the cab of the truck and tossed her carry-on over my shoulder. I figured I'd come back for her other stuff after I got her settled in my room.

"Sunshine," I growled to get her attention. She

turned narrowed eyes on me, and I tilted my head toward a path that led to the clubhouse front door. I waited for her to march past me, then followed her, my eyes glued to her spectacular ass.

When we reached the front door, she slammed it open and stomped inside. I ambled in after her, trying not to give away the tension that gripped me when I saw how many brothers had their eyes on my girl.

"I want to speak to whoever is in charge!" Karina demanded loudly, planting her hands on her hips and darting her gaze around the large lounge.

"Relax, sunshine," I muttered. "You'll get your questions answered, just like I promised. For now, let's get you settled."

I knew Mac would want to meet first to go over everything that had happened and talk about next steps.

So I was grateful when Cat, our VP's old lady, came out from behind the bar and sauntered over to us with a welcoming smile.

"You must be Karina," she said with a wink. "I'm Cat, your tour guide and safety director. If you follow me, I'll take you to your room." Before turning away, Cat shot me a questioning glance, silently asking me if she should take my girl to my room. I nodded, and she started talking to Karina as she led her away.

I watched them until they'd disappeared up the stairs, then the outraged voice of another tiny woman drew my attention away when she stalked over to me with a thunderous expression.

"What do you think you're doing, Cash?" Kiara snapped.

Irritated as fuck, I turned to glare at her. If she thought she was going to come between Karina and me, she was in for a rude awakening. However, Knight was right on her heels, and when he saw my expression, his brow furrowed in warning. Respectful of my brother's old lady, I scaled back my anger.

Kiara wagged her finger at me and continued, "You can't—"

"Baby," Knight interrupted once he caught up with her. He tucked her under his arm and bent his head to whisper in her ear. "You can't get involved." He was just loud enough that I heard what he was saying. *Damn straight.*

"But—"

"If he's decided that she's his, we will not get involved," he said more firmly. "Promise me."

I trusted Knight to handle his woman, so I turned and stalked down the hall to the prez's office.

He looked up when he heard me approaching and leaned back in his chair, watching me with a neutral expression. Mac was never easy to read.

He lifted his chin when I neared, giving me permission to enter. I dropped down on the couch to my left and put my feet up on the low table in front of me.

"That your woman making all that noise?" he asked.

I grunted, and he smirked. "Gonna have your hands full."

"No shit," I muttered. "You hear anything on Bickle?" I asked, changing the subject. I wasn't ready to talk about Karina. I was still getting used to the feelings of possession and my growing obsession for the little spitfire.

"We've got a few leads. I think one of these will pan out. Probably gonna catch up with him in the next day or two."

"I want in. She's mine."

Mac nodded. "Done."

He was filling me in on the details when Scout, the VP, came in with a message from an informant. We discussed the tip and whether it was a legitimate lead. When Knight also showed up, he shot me a look that I returned with a nod, then he joined the conversation.

Once we wrapped up our business, I stood and made my way over to Mac's desk. "What can I tell her?" I'd followed his instructions while on the road. But now that we were here and I knew just what Karina was to me, I didn't want anyone else answering her questions.

"Anything that doesn't involve club business."

I lifted my chin in acknowledgment but didn't say anything because Mac's phone rang. When he picked up the call, his entire demeanor went soft, indicating that it was his old lady. It would be startling for most people to see the big, mean-looking MC president turn into a marshmallow. But we'd all learned early on not to give him shit about it because that softness only extended to his wife and children.

I walked out of the office and spotted Knight waiting for me, lounging against the wall. He lifted his chin toward another office, and we stepped inside to talk.

"I'm not going to push her," I said without preamble.

"Kiara is anxious as shit about the situation, and I don't like seeing her unhappy."

I crossed my arms over my chest and scowled at him. "She's barely had time to process that her dad is a fucking asshole, let alone that she has a sister. Especially when that sister is the one who kept her dad from being with her all this time and committing to her mom. She's gonna get as much time as she needs, brother. But you can tell Kiara that I think Karina will be ready eventually."

Knight looked like he wanted to push further, but after a few seconds, he pressed his lips together and gave me a chin lift before flipping around and stalking from the room.

I was suddenly exhausted and just wanted to crawl into bed with my girl and sleep for a day. As I headed for the stairs, I paused by the entrance to the kitchen. Karina was probably hungry. I'd offered to stop for food on the way from the airport, but the stubborn woman just ordered me to hurry up and get to where we were going.

Maybe a snack would be the perfect peace offering. Now that Karina was under lock and key, I wasn't going to pussyfoot around the fact that she was mine.

After rummaging around in the huge communal pantry and fridge, I found some decent snacks and carried them up to my room.

Since I was single and managed the garage attached to the clubhouse, I hadn't bothered to find my own place. That would have to change now, but I'd wait until after we put Bickle in the ground. Then Karina could decide where she wanted to live, as long as it was with me.

I hadn't expected to find my sunshine asleep in my bed when I came to the room, but I wasn't surprised, considering the day we'd had.

After setting the snacks on the nightstand, I stripped to my boxers and climbed into bed. Karina rolled toward me, and I smiled at the proof that she was drawn to me, whether she wanted to admit it or not. I hooked my arm around her waist and pulled her close, then wrapped my body around hers and fell into a contented sleep.

I wasn't sure what I'd expected to happen when I arrived at the Silver Saints compound, but it wasn't to be shown to a room and pass out before I had the chance to speak to their president...let alone to wake up with Cash wrapped around me.

Turning in his embrace, I stared at his gorgeous face. My fingers itched to trace every inch of his tanned skin. I wanted to rub my palm against the dark scruff of his beard. And to press my lips against his. Except he looked so peaceful in his sleep, I didn't want to interrupt his rest. Not to mention I didn't want my first kiss to be with a man who wasn't awake to enjoy it. Especially not after he'd basically dragged me to his MC's compound and abandoned me.

Instead, I slid out of his hold and crawled off the

mattress to head into the bathroom. After washing up, I stared at my reflection in the mirror and whispered, "What the heck?"

I didn't understand why my body had decided now was the perfect time for my libido to come roaring to life. My life was a mess, and I was being forced to hide so the guy who wanted revenge on my dad didn't kill me. The last thing I needed was the complication of falling for the biker who'd been tasked with keeping me safe by his president. No matter how sexy he was. Or how often I'd spotted the heat of desire in his dark eyes when he looked at me.

After taking a few deep breaths, I pressed my thighs together in a futile attempt to squash the unfamiliar ache in my core caused by waking up with Cash's arms around me, then I headed out of the bathroom. Now that I was fully awake and had cleared most of the sensual fog, I spotted something I'd missed earlier...Cash had brought me a snack when he'd come to the room last night.

While the plate of food could have come from someone else, I had no doubt it was him since there wasn't a single item on it that I didn't like. The only other person who knew my preferences so well was my mom, but there was no way it could've been her.

Even before I learned about my dad's other

family, he hadn't modeled the male side of a healthy relationship for me. I had never doubted that he loved my mom—until now—but he was gone so often that she'd had to take care of herself. She was the one who handled everything—grocery shopping, house cleaning and repairs, car maintenance, lawn care, rolling the garbage cans out to the curb. She kept our lives running without any assistance from him except financial.

I'd never really seen a man care for a woman until Cash started doing it for me. Making sure I could stay at the cabin over the holiday even though he wanted us to come back here, where he was certain I'd be safe. Feeding me. Making hot chocolate.

As frustrated as I was over not having all of my questions answered—and still more than a little irritated over how Cash had given me no choice about leaving the cabin—I still appreciated everything he'd done for me. My reaction to him gave his actions deeper meaning. The snack he'd prepared for me tasted even sweeter because he'd gone out of his way to take care of me again.

As I was finishing a plump strawberry, my head jerked up at the rumble of a deep voice. "Morning, sunshine. Glad to see you found the food. I was worried that you were hungry last night, but you were passed the fuck out when I got up here, so I figured you could use the rest more than food."

"I definitely woke up hungry." And not just for food.

"What were you thinking about while you were eating?" The sheet dropped as he sat up, and my cheeks heated when I realized the only reason it didn't move lower was because it snagged on the large bulge between his legs. "It looked like you had the weight of the world on your shoulders."

"It was so strange to think that I have my dad's awful decisions to thank for bringing you into my life. Without them, we probably never would have met." My reaction to his hard-on was to blame for my honesty, but I couldn't regret what I'd said when I saw the gleam of happiness in his eyes.

He brushed away a lock of dark hair that fell over his eye as he shook his head. "You're wrong. I have no doubt our paths would've crossed at some point."

I quirked a brow. "Even though I live in a different state?"

"Yup." He beckoned me over to him. "C'mere, sunshine. I wanna see how good those strawberries taste."

Lifting one off the plate, I brought it over to him.

But instead of taking it from me, he wrapped his hand around the back of my head to tug me closer. When my knees bumped against the side of the bed, I fell against his chest. Then he drew me against him and rolled over until my back was against the mattress, and he hovered over me. "I thought you said you wanted a strawberry?"

"There's a better way for me to see how they taste." His lips curved into a smile of pure, masculine satisfaction at my look of confusion. "From your lips since you just had one."

"Oh," I breathed.

He lowered his head slowly, letting me decide whether we were going to kiss now. Any doubts I might have had were wiped away in an instant over how careful he was being with me. Cash had been with me for all but the first few hours since my dad's secrets had shattered my world. After feeling so helpless, having him give me the power at this moment meant...everything. "Yes, please."

His mouth crashed down against mine, his tongue swiping against me, demanding entrance. My lips parted, and I moaned when it slid inside. My eyes drifted shut as he devoured me, tilted my head to the side so he could deepen the kiss that left me breathless and dazed when he finally pulled away.

"Wow," I whispered, pressing my fingers to my tingling lips.

"Damn, I should've kissed you that first day instead of giving you time to come to terms with the shit your dad laid on you. We could've been doing this instead of watching all those sappy holiday movies. Bet it would've put you in a much better mood."

I wished we could stay in this bed and ignore the outside world, just the two of us. I wanted to explore the magnetic pull I felt toward Cash—the man who'd just given me my first real kiss. Unfortunately, I had questions that needed answers. "I hate to say it, but we're going to need to wait to do that again. I want to talk to Mac. Now."

6

CASH

I captured Karina's chin between my thumb and forefinger, forcing her gaze to meet mine. "Mac might be my president, but when it comes to you, sunshine, I'm in charge."

A little shiver skated down her body, and I grinned, about to say something guaranteed to make her blush, when there was a knock on the door.

Grumbling, I planted a quick kiss on Karina's lips before rolling off her and getting to my feet. Then I padded over to yell at whoever was interrupting my time with my girl.

Knight was standing in the hall, arms crossed, feet spread apart and giving me his most intimidating glare. I mirrored his stance and scowled right back at him.

"Told you to back off, Knight."

"Kiara wants to meet her sister."

"I haven't had a chance to explain shit to her, brother. She needs some time. I'll let you know when and if she decides she wants to meet her sister."

Knight's expression darkened even further. "It's gonna happen Cash. I won't have Kiara disappointed and hurt by this. Once they meet, they can make up their own minds about where to take it from there. But they won't know until they fucking meet!"

I stepped into the hall and shut the door. "Told you before, I don't doubt it's gonna happen, but you gotta give her some damn time to process. Kiara has had a fuck of a lot more time to let all this shit sink in."

Some of the tension in Knight dissipated, and I knew my next comment would win the argument. "If the roles were reversed, what would you do?"

Knight unfolded his arms and grunted. "I'll try to keep Kiara busy...but before long, she'll be here banging on your door herself."

"Don't you have control of your woman, Knight?" I drawled, just to piss him off.

"Give it a day, Cash. You'll be as pussy whipped as every other Saint with property."

He was probably right, so I let it go. "I'll call," I said one last time before re-entering my room.

Karina stood in the middle of the room, twisting her hands together and staring at the door.

"My sister is here? She wants to meet me?"

"Your sister belongs to one of my brothers," I explained as I prowled toward her. When I was a foot away, I grasped her wrist and walked her over to the small sofa at the end of the room. I sat down and pulled her onto my lap, then got her settled before finally continuing. "When all this bullshit started, Kiara showed up here"—I cracked a smile when I thought about Knight describing his first encounter with Kiara because it reminded me of Karina—"A lot like you. Fired up, determined to talk to the prez. She'd just found out what your dad had been accused of." I went on to give her a quick version of Kiara and Knight's story, everything that went down with Bickle, and then when the judge finally admitted to Kiara that she had a sister.

"So...that's why Mac was willing to protect me after what my dad had done to your friend? Another member of the club?"

I nodded and looked straight into her eyes when I spoke. "Silver Saints aren't angels. We do a lotta good, but our methods are questionable or outright wrong to a lot of people. We follow our own law and have our own brand of justice. You understand what I'm getting at, sunshine?"

She nodded slowly but didn't speak.

"We also protect our women by any means necessary. If someone threatens one of our old ladies, they are diggin' their own grave 'cause when we catch up to them, they won't be breathing much longer. Kiara is Knight's old lady. That means she has the protection of every man who wears our insignia. And, by extension, you."

"Mac...he sent you just because we're related?"

"No, baby. He sent me because Kiara would never have forgiven Knight, or any of us, if we hadn't done everything in our power to keep you safe. From the moment she found out about you, her first instinct was to protect you. Like an older sister should."

"Okay. I guess I should go—"

I placed a finger over her lips. "No. Not should, sunshine. You don't gotta do anything you don't want to. If you aren't ready, hell, if you aren't ever ready, I'll take the heat."

Karina's shoulders lost some of their tension, and her eyes were soft as she blinked up at me. "That's the sweetest thing anyone has ever said to me."

I frowned and growled playfully, "You tell anyone I said somethin' sweet, and I'm gonna tie you to the bed and drive you wild without letting you break until you promise to behave."

Heat flared in her eyes, and the semi I was already sporting around her became a full-fledged erection. It grew under her ass, and there was no way she didn't feel it.

Her cheeks flushed with pink, and she licked her lips, making me emit a tortured groan. "You better decide what you want to do fast, sunshine. Or I'm going to take you back to that bed and see just how wet it makes you when I talk dirty."

Karina looked indecisive, and since all I wanted was to be buried inside her, it was a true miracle that I managed to push past my lust to be logical.

When I finally got Karina under me, I didn't want this shit hanging over our heads or Knight interrupting us again.

"Do you want to meet her, sunshine?"

Karina didn't hesitate, at first. "Yes." Then she paused, and I studied her as she worked something out in her mind.

When she continued to be silent, I prompted her, "Talk to me."

"What if she blames me for everything? I mean,

my mom is the 'other' woman. What if she hates me?"

"Never gonna happen, sunshine. I know Kiara, and she isn't like that."

"But it's not like you've seen her in this situation before. What if this is—"

"Karina." I said her name firmly, cutting off her babbling worries and bringing her full attention to me. "I guarantee you that Kiara understands your side of things. She's excited to have a sister."

I bent my head and pressed a kiss to her lips, then collared her neck with my hand, rubbing my thumb softly over her skin. "If I'm wrong, then I'll be right there beside you."

She looked deeply into my eyes, as if searching for something. She must have found whatever it was because she sighed and laid her head on my chest. "Why would you do this for me?" she asked softly.

I threaded my fingers through her hair and tugged until her head was back far enough that she was looking up into my face. "Haven't you been listening, sunshine? Because you're mine."

7

KARINA

I probably should have been worried about how quickly Cash was becoming so important to me —especially right after my dad had proven how untrustworthy he was. But it wasn't fair to make Cash pay for the mistakes someone else had made when he'd been so supportive of me.

My knees were shaking so hard that I wasn't sure I would have made it down the hallway to meet the half sister I'd never known if Cash hadn't been by my side. With his arm around my shoulders, he guided me to an apartment outside the clubhouse and above a workshop. Apparently, it was where Kiara and Knight lived. Before he rapped his knuckles against the hard surface of the door, he turned to me.

Pressing a finger under my chin to tilt my head back, he scanned my expression and asked, "Ready?"

"I guess I better be. That Knight guy didn't look like he was going to take no for an answer."

He stroked his hand down my back. "Like I said, nobody's gonna make you do anything you don't want."

I flashed him a soft smile. "I know, it's just my nerves talking."

He brushed his lips against mine. "She's gonna love you."

I hoped he was right, but there wasn't any more time to worry because as soon as he knocked, the door was flung open and a woman—who I probably would've guessed was related to me if we'd met under different circumstances because we looked so much alike—threw herself at me. "I'm so glad you're finally here, baby sister."

"Baby sister?" I echoed with a giggle, wrapping my arms around her back and giving her the biggest hug I'd ever given anyone as my eyes filled with tears. I'd never been much of a crier until the past few days, but nobody could blame me since my life had been turned upside down. At least these were happy ones.

Tears streamed down Kiara's cheeks when she

took a step back. "I'm a whole year older than you, so that makes me your big sister."

"True, but can we stick with little instead?" I asked, my nose wrinkling. "I'm eighteen, too old to be a baby anything."

"I don't mind calling you little sister, but you're wrong about that." She flashed a grin over her shoulder. "Tell her what you call me all the time."

"Whatever you want, baby," Knight murmured as he tugged her against his chest, wrapping his arms around her stomach as he stared at us over the top of her head.

"Okay, but that's totally different." I jerked my chin toward Cash. "Although he calls me sunshine instead of baby."

Kiara's eyes narrowed. "I'm not sure how I feel about that."

Knight shook his head with a chuckle. "Did you already forget your promise about not getting involved?"

"No, but that was before I met my sister," she huffed.

Knowing that they'd been talking about what was happening between Cash and me had my cheeks filling with heat. Since that was a subject I wanted to avoid until I knew exactly what was going on with us, I blurted, "Um, so...you're not mad about me?"

"Not at all," Kiara assured as she stepped away from Knight to tug me into the room. "Being an only child kind of sucked for me, so I always wished I had a sibling."

She led me over to the recliner in the corner before perching on the side of the mattress closest to me. "I didn't mind that much since I've known my best friend for so long that it's basically like we're sisters."

Kiara beamed a smile at me. "Tell me all about her."

"Her name is Lorelei." I shot a glare at Cash, who was leaning against the doorway. "I'm not sure where she is right now since she was on vacation with me in Aspen. Kidnapping must be popular with the Silver Saints because some guy named Grey apparently snatched her when she came back from skiing the day that my...*our* dad told me what was going on."

Kiara didn't look the slightest bit surprised. "Yeah, I guess it makes sense for the guys not to shy away from kidnapping when the president and his old lady got together when he took her from her bedroom in a rival club's compound years ago."

"Really?" I gasped, my eyes widening.

"Yup." Her attention shifted to Knight and Cash, and she made a shooing motion with her hands. "I think we'll be fine by ourselves for a little bit, guys. You might as well find something to do while we do some sisterly bonding over gossip."

"Don't go anywhere until I'm back," Cash grumbled as Knight bumped his shoulder to force him into the hallway before shutting the door behind them.

"Where would I even go?" I muttered, shaking my head.

"They tend to be ridiculously overprotective." She rolled her eyes—the same shade of blue as mine—with a laugh. "They'll probably be waiting right outside the door the whole time we're talking, just in case one of us needs something."

"He probably thought he was just being protective when he tossed me over his shoulder for 'my own good' when I didn't want to leave Aspen," I muttered.

"I'm not surprised at all. That Bickle guy is scary." She pressed her lips together and shivered. "But I don't want to ruin our first conversation by talking about any of the bad stuff right off the bat."

Telling me about how Mac and Bridget became a couple was the perfect way to break the ice. Once that story was done, I felt as though I'd known Kiara for years instead of minutes. Maybe the instant connection between us was because we were sisters. I couldn't be sure, but it didn't really matter. I was just happy we were bonding.

After she told me a few more stories about how some of the other couples got together, I asked her about Knight. That got us talking about the stuff that had gone down with our dad since that's how they met. "Bickle really broke Dad's hand? He didn't say anything about that when he called Mom and me in Aspen."

"Yeah, I was hiding in the closet in his office when it happened." She cringed. "It was awful."

"I'm so sorry you had to go through that." I leaned over so I could pat her hand, offering her a tremulous smile when she flipped her arm over to lace our fingers together and squeezed.

"It was totally worth it to meet Knight and finally find out about you."

My voice was shaky when I asked, "Um, what about your mom? How's she taking everything?"

"I'm not really sure." Kiara shrugged with a sigh. "We've barely talked since everything went down, and she jetted off to some tropical island for Christmas because she couldn't bear to be in town over the holidays knowing that people were gossiping about Dad."

My eyes widened. "Didn't she want you to go with her? It's Christmas!"

"Nope, she was almost as mad at me for getting together with Shane as she was with Dad for getting caught sending innocent people to jail." She shook her head with a shrug. "She's always been more concerned about appearances than my happiness. She was already gone before I found out about you and plans to stay a while. I don't know if Dad has even told her yet."

"Yikes." It was a relief to hear that my dad's wife was as awful as he'd told us because that meant he wasn't lying, at least not about that. And I didn't have to feel quite so guilty about him loving my mom instead of Kiara's. But it was also horrible because I hated that Kiara hadn't gotten to grow up with a mom like mine. "I'm sorry."

"None of this is your fault, Karina." She got up and pulled me to my feet so she could give me another hug. "This situation sucks for both of us, but at least we have each other to lean on now."

I beamed a smile at her. "Yeah, we do."

She was probably right about the guys waiting right outside the door since Cash chose that moment to poke his head inside to ask, "You guys okay?"

"Better than okay," I chirped.

"We're awesome," Kiara added.

Knight came inside and pulled my sister against his side as Cash led me into the hallway and back to his room.

"Thank you, thank you, thank you," I chanted, gripping his shoulders as I pressed my cheek against his chest once the door shut behind us.

His palm slid down my spine, sending a sensual shiver in its wake. "For what, sunshine?"

"Everything," I breathed.

"Even though you haven't gotten the chance to talk to Mac yet?"

"Uh-huh." I nodded. "Getting to know my sister was way more important, and she filled me in on a lot of what went down."

A gleam of humor shone in his eyes as he asked, "Does your thank-you include me kidnapping you?"

Thinking about the stories my sister had shared with me, I nodded. "Especially that."

"Thank fuck. I figured you'd be pissed at me over that for a long damn time."

I pressed my hands against the back of his neck so he'd lean closer as I whispered, "Nope."

Then I threw caution to the wind and kissed him. It was fantastic...right up until the point when he ripped his mouth from mine with a deep groan.

Jumping away from him, I dropped my gaze to my feet as heat filled my cheeks and tears welled in my eyes. "I'm sorry. I figured since you kissed me earlier that...um...you'd be okay with me kissing you, too. I guess I misunderstood."

"You think I don't want you, sunshine?" I asked incredulously. I couldn't believe this perfect angel of a woman didn't realize how badly I wanted her. My cock was rock hard just from grinding into her center during our make-out session. "Karina, I want you more than anything I've wanted in my entire life. But I'm not going to rush you."

She looked relieved, even though her cheeks flamed with color, and she ducked her eyes.

"I...um...want..."

My breath caught in my lungs as hope sprung up inside me. I lifted her chin with one finger until our gazes locked. "Tell me, sunshine. What do you want?"

She took a deep breath, then whispered, "You. I want to be with you."

I closed my eyes and tried not to lose my fucking mind. Once I felt like I wouldn't pounce, I opened them back up and let her see the raw hunger burning inside. There was no reason to hide it any longer. "You're a fucking goddess, sunshine, you know that?" I murmured as I bent down and nuzzled her neck before slowly pushing her sweater up over her tits and taking it off over her head.

The thin cups of her pink lacy bra barely contained her breasts. My mouth watered, and my lips tingled. I was going to die if I didn't taste them as soon as possible.

Kissing down her neck and over the fabric, I sucked in a nipple through the lacy material.

She moaned and bucked her hips, rubbing her pussy harder against me. Despite the layers between us, I could feel the intense heat from her sex, and I bet she was soaked.

"Cash," she whimpered.

"Tell me what you want, sunshine."

"I...I don't know. I've never...never done this before."

I pulled my mouth from her breast and stared

down at her. Surely, I hadn't heard my beautiful girl right. "You've never done what, Karina?"

She shook her head, her teeth catching her plump bottom lip. "Um, I—I've never had sex. I'm a virgin."

My heart thudded against my chest. "I'm your first?"

She nodded. "If that's okay."

"Oh, sunshine, that's more than okay," I rasped, caressing her cheek with the back of my hand. "But now I know I gotta take care of this pussy before you're able to handle my cock."

I couldn't wait for another second, so I quickly yanked off her jeans and pink panties.

Her pussy was bare, the lips glistening with her arousal. I licked my lips and buried my nose between her legs, inhaling deeply. "You smell fucking delicious."

Her breathing sped up as I rested my hands on her thighs and pushed them wider so I could nuzzle her slick folds.

She gasped, and I licked up the cream that gushed from her pussy. I'd barely touched her, but I could tell she was already nearly there. Eager to see her fall apart, I drove my tongue inside her, then licked up and around her clit before spearing her channel again. She held my hair with a grip so tight it stung, but the small prick of pain only added to my growing need.

Growling into her pussy, I wrapped my big hands around her thighs and gripped them firmly as I pulled her closer. Soon, that sweet little body was writhing on my face.

"Cash, I...oh, yes...I'm gonna come," she whispered breathlessly.

I released one of her legs and slid a finger into her tight-as-fuck pussy. Shit, I was going to have to work her hard to make sure I didn't break her when I finally got inside.

Hooking my digit inside her, I sucked her clit hard in my mouth. Her orgasm hit hard and fast as her pussy walls shuddered around my finger. But I wanted more. Every climax would soften her and make it a little easier when I filled her with my big cock.

I popped my lips off her clit long enough to say, "Give me another one, sunshine. I want your taste to drench my tongue when you come. Don't hold back. Want to hear you screaming my name."

I went back to devouring her. She hadn't fully recovered from the first orgasm, but I didn't wait to go back in. I managed to work in two fingers this time, and I stretched her tight little pussy as I swirled my tongue around her clit, working her primed body into a frenzy.

"Oh, Cash! Yes!" she shouted, grinding against my face. "I'm coming again! Yes! Yes!"

A few seconds later, she pressed her head back into the pillow and screamed my name as she rode my face, squirting her juices down my throat. I lapped up every last drop while doing everything I could to hold back my own orgasm. Once the eye of the storm had passed, her body was still pulsing, but her limbs flopped down onto the mattress as if she'd gone boneless. The expression on her face made my groin tighten to the point of pain. She was staring at the ceiling with a look of awe and bliss.

"Never seen anything more beautiful than watching you come for me, sunshine," I grunted. "I can't wait to see you do it on my cock."

I jumped up from the bed and pulled at my clothes, but I was on edge, and my shaking hands struggled to unsnap my jeans. Then I stumbled when I toed off my boots, making Karina giggle. It was such a magical sound that I didn't give a fuck how ridiculous I must have looked.

When I had stripped down to my boxers, her eyes locked on the tent between my legs. I slowly dragged my underwear down, being careful not to catch the fabric on my dick. I was so damn hard that the slightest pressure caused me pain. Karina sat up, and her mouth formed a little O, her eyes going wide and round. When I climbed back onto the bed, she was face-to-face with my long, thick cock. It bobbed against my stomach, and the purple, angry-looking tip was shiny with precome.

"Um...I don't think that's going to fit in me," she breathed, blinking her big blue eyes.

I leaned forward, forcing her to lie back again, and hovered over her on my hands and knees. "Sunshine," I grunted, "this pussy was made for me. Only me."

Her bottom lip quivered, and I sucked it between my teeth, nibbling the succulent flesh.

After a second, she pulled away, but only long enough to press our mouths together. She kissed me deeply, wrapping her arms and legs around me as I lowered my body down over hers. Everywhere our skin touched, I sizzled with passion and need.

My cock was cradled in the apex of her thighs, and when I moved my hips, she was so wet that I slid between her pussy lips. Karina moaned, and her head pressed into the mattress while her legs clamped tighter around me.

"Fuck," I muttered. "You feel so damn good. So hot."

I moved back just enough to position my dick at her entrance.

When Karina felt the tip at her channel, she bucked her hips, taking it inside her. "Oh, Cash! That feels..."

"What does it feel like, sunshine?" I demanded as I circled my hips and pushed in a few more centimeters. "Tell me."

"More. Like I need more," she breathed.

My balls were already tightening, so I paused and tried to regain some control. It wasn't easy with her juices already coating my cock. I took a deep, calming breath before claiming Karina's lips in a kiss, devouring her mouth as I pushed in a little farther. She was tight. So fucking tight. Squeezing me hard enough that there was a bite of pain, which sent even more blood rushing to my groin.

Finally, I felt the thin barrier that would make Karina mine in every way. I was gonna be the first, last, and only man to see her like this. Touch her like this. Be inside her.

I dragged my mouth away and growled, "This sweet cherry is mine, Karina. I'm gonna pop it and make you mine."

She licked her lips and stared into my eyes, clearly nervous, but her blue orbs were also filled with excitement.

"Please," she whispered.

I nodded and nudged the barrier once more. "Relax, baby. Gonna try not to hurt you."

She tensed, but then I slipped a hand between us and played with her clit as I slowly drew my hips back. When she was moaning and writhing beneath me, I pistoned my hips and tore through her virginity. I had intended to stop and give her time before working my big dick all the way in, but knowing what I'd done and what it meant, coupled with the grip of her walls around my shaft, was too much for my brain to process.

"Fuck!" I shouted as I slammed in until I was so deep that I bumped her cervix.

Karina cried out, and the sound broke through my haze of passion, enough for me to keep still and check to make sure she was okay. "Sunshine?"

Karina's breaths were choppy, making her tits bounce enticingly, and I bent down to lick around one nipple before sucking on it like it was candy.

"Cash," she whimpered.

Worried, I released her nipple with a pop and looked up at her face. I'd expected it to be twisted in a painful grimace, but instead, she was biting her lip and watching me with pleading eyes.

"You okay?" I gritted, still struggling to stay focused on her and not the way it felt for my bare cock to be buried balls deep in her virgin pussy.

"No," she mumbled, making my heart stop. "I need you to move."

Oh fuck, yeah. "Whatever you want," I told her as I withdrew, then drove back in.

Karina's shout of ecstasy nearly caused me to explode, but I was determined to make her come before I let go.

I repeated my actions, moving rhythmically as my pace increased until I pounded in and out of her pussy. "Fuck, Karina. Oh yeah. Squeeze that pussy. You feel so damn good wrapped around my cock."

Suddenly, Karina froze, and I paused for a second to see what had caused it. "I'm not on the pill," she panted.

"Good," I rumbled as I picked up my pace again.

"Cash!" she gasped. "You could get me pregnant...oh! Oh!" She ended her warning with a cry of ecstasy when I shifted my position so I went even deeper and glided over her clit every time I went in and out.

"So?"

Karina smacked my shoulder, then immediately grabbed it, digging her nails into my skin as she began to meet me thrust for thrust. "You...oh, yes... Cash...you should probably pull out."

"Not a fucking chance in hell, sunshine," I growled as I grabbed the headboard for leverage and fucked her hard and fast. The more she talked about me knocking her up, the more my hunger grew. "Not gonna leave this tight little pussy until I've filled you with so much come that I'll be leaking out of you for days. And every time you feel it, you'll know who you belong to."

"Don't stop! Oh yes! Yes!" Karina yelled as her body shook with the need to come. She was close, and it was a damn good thing because I wouldn't last much longer.

"Come for me, sunshine."

Karina screamed as she came on my cock, dragging me over the edge with her.

"Fuck! Karina!" I bellowed as I exploded inside her and my hot come splashed against her walls. "That's it, baby. Milk my cock. Be a good little girl and take every drop. Fuck, yes!"

It took a hell of a lot longer than I expected to empty all of my seed into her waiting womb. It was as if my body just kept making the stuff, knowing it would give us the best chance of putting a baby in her belly.

As we drifted back down to reality, I kissed each of her tits, her neck, cheeks, eyelids, and then took her mouth in a deep, soul-binding kiss.

I was shocked when her body tightened around me again, and I realized that I was still hard as a fucking rock. Karina moaned and glided her hands down my chest and around my back to clutch my ass.

"You up for more, sunshine?" I asked dubiously. The last thing I wanted to do was hurt her any more than I'd been forced to.

"Uh-huh, need more," she panted, her nails digging into my flesh, sending streaks of pleasure straight to my core.

I was afraid I'd lose control if I took her like this again, so I asked, "You wanna ride me, sunshine?"

She smiled shyly and nodded, making me grin at the eagerness in her baby blues. I flipped onto my back, and she straddled my hips, resting her hands on my chest as she stared down at me wide-eyed and unsure.

I cupped her hips and guided her up and down. "Do what feels good, baby. You're in charge. Fuck me."

She stilled for a moment, then a spark of power

glinted in her light orbs before she slowly lifted, then fell back down and ground herself against me.

"Oh, fuck yeah," I groaned.

She started to move faster, growing more frenzied and desperate until she was practically bouncing on my cock. Her big, gorgeous tits danced in my face, and I cupped them, giving the globes a squeeze before twisting and plucking her nipples.

She dropped her head back, moaning as she rocked harder against my cock. "Yesssss."

"Fuck, you feel so good, sunshine. So fucking good."

"Oh god, Cash."

I grinned as it hit me that every time I talked dirty to her, the walls of her pussy would clamp down on my cock.

"You like it when I say filthy things to you?"

Her cheeks turned pink, but she nodded, making me proud of her for admitting what she liked and asking for more.

I moved my hands to her ass and palmed her cheeks, slamming her down every time I bucked up. I raised my head and watched our connection in fascination. "I'm so fucking deep inside you, baby. This pussy was made for me to eat, to fuck, to fill you with my come."

She moaned as her body writhed above me. "Yes, Cash."

"Yeah, that's it, sunshine. Come all over my cock. Come hard for me, baby." I slipped a hand between us and rubbed her hard bundle of nerves.

That was all it took, her walls tightened around my cock, and she threw her head back and screamed my name with each buck of her hips. As she rode out her orgasm, I rolled her onto her back and wrapped her legs around my waist. I pumped hard and fast, feeling her hard nipples brush against my chest hair.

"Say my name, sunshine," I growled.

"Cash," she moaned.

"Call my name while I fill this pretty pussy with my come."

"Oh, Cash, oh fuck, Cash!"

With those words, I shoved my cock in as deep as I possibly could. My come spurted out in thick jets, setting off another climax in Karina.

Once my balls were empty, I didn't have any energy left. I collapsed on top of Karina, though I was careful not to crush her. I couldn't move. I was too content to...I didn't know what. The feelings she inspired were unknown territory for me. This driving need to knock her up, to make sure she was tied to me in every way—should have scared the fuck out of me. Instead, I felt like I was exactly where I was supposed to be.

After a few minutes, I rolled onto my back, taking her with me and keeping my cock snug and warm inside her. We stayed intertwined as our shallow breaths evened out and eventually drifted off to sleep.

9

I was amazed by how quickly I'd adjusted to living in an MC compound...and losing my virginity. After we broke the seal, so to speak, Cash and I spent most of the day in bed together. We only had sex twice more—because he'd been worried about me getting too sore—and spent the rest of the time talking about anything and everything. With the exception of the one thing I was too chicken to mention. Cash had refused to pull out every time we'd had sex. And it seemed almost as though he was trying to get me pregnant...unless it was just stuff said in the heat of the moment. I hadn't worked up the courage to ask, though.

I'd learned that his road name was his childhood nickname, not too far off from Cassius. Since Cash was already really darn cool, he'd convinced the guys that he didn't need a new name back when he finished prospecting for the club—another thing he'd explained to me. I was impressed by the fact that he managed their auto shop and was in awe of the classic car restorations he'd shown me that his friend Dom had done.

Someone brought up a tray of food around noon, so we hadn't left his room until dinnertime. When my stomach growled, he'd dragged me out of bed and downstairs to the kitchen, and we'd found a dozen people seated at the tables, digging into three large pans of lasagna and piles of garlic bread. Sharing a meal had given me a chance to get to know several of Cash's club brothers and their old ladies—a term that my sister had explained was in no way meant to be derogatory, even though it sounded like it to outsiders.

Seeing how these big, strong men catered to their women convinced me that she was right. And made me hope for a day in the future when Cash and I were as in sync as the other couples we'd eaten with.

All that time together yesterday—plus those days in Aspen even though we hadn't really talked then—was like stringing a bunch of dates back-to-back. It made me feel as though we'd been together for much longer than the week since we'd met. And I was already falling head over heels in love with Cash. Not that I'd said those three little words out loud yet. It was way too soon for that. But I had reached the point when I trusted him enough to ask for what I needed.

Shifting in his embrace so I was looking at him instead of the show we were watching while cuddled up in bed together, I murmured, "I want to see my mom and dad."

He stroked his thumb across my cheek. "You sure you're ready for that?"

"I want to make sure my mom is okay. She was completely in love with my dad, and I don't know how things went down with him when she left Aspen." I heaved a deep sigh. "And if I'm being completely honest with myself...even though my dad made such terrible mistakes and I'm so, so pissed at him, I still love him. I'm not ready to forgive him. I'm not sure if I ever will be, but I'd like to see him. Especially if my mom kicked him to the curb." I stopped for a second and swallowed hard, pushing back the tears threatening to spill over. This whole situation was an emotional roller coaster, but I knew I could take these steps with Cash by my side. "Besides, I'm not sure how many opportunities I'm going to have to see my dad without bars between us."

"I get why you feel like it needs to be now, and I'm willing to arrange it, so long as you understand that the meet would have to happen here," he reminded me.

"Yeah, I figured." I stroked my palm up his bare chest. "You've made it very clear that I can't leave until you guys find Bickle, and I have no desire to get caught by someone who wants to kill me."

"No fucking way will I ever let that bastard get his hands on you," Cash growled before dipping his head to capture my lips in a deep kiss.

It took me a minute to catch my breath when he finished. "I know you won't let anything happen to me."

"Damn straight." He twisted around to grab his cell off the bedside table. "And that includes your dad pulling any shit that hurts you during your talk. I'm gonna be there to make sure he doesn't fuck up any more than he already has."

"Okay." No way in heck was I going to argue with that order when I wanted him by my side anyway. Seeing my dad for the first time after finding out what he'd hidden from me was going to be hard.

"I like when my sunshine is agreeable." He gave

me another quick kiss, then tapped a few messages out on his phone. "Mac gave his okay for your parents to drop by to see you. Do you want me to set it up with your dad? Or do you want to ask?"

I didn't want to talk to my dad until we were face-to-face. I needed time to figure out what I wanted to say and to see his expression when he answered my questions. "You, please."

"Before that," Cash stopped for a second as he leaned forward and shrugged out of his cut. "Need to make a statement that can't be missed, sunshine." He slipped my arms through the holes of his vest, and I felt the weight of the leather as it settled on my shoulders. "What's that?"

"You're mine."

His possessive words stuck with me as we made our way downstairs. My dad had agreed to come over right away, so I hadn't needed to wait long.

Nobody was in the large area, not even at the bar even though it was a Friday night. "Thanks for making sure we had some privacy for this."

"Always gonna make sure you have what you need, sunshine." He led me over to one of the couches and got me settled, standing guard next to me with his fists at his hips. "My brothers understood how important this meeting was to you."

"Oh no. I should've asked Kiara if she wanted to join us."

Cash shook his head. "Don't worry about your sister. Knight is aware that your dad is gonna be here any minute. If she wanted to see him, she'd be down here already."

"Yeah, I guess you're right."

"No guessing needed."

Before I could tease him about being so cocky, the door opened, and my parents walked into the clubhouse. I resisted the urge to jump up and run toward them. Instead, I just stood and focused on my mom as they crossed the room. Considering the situation, I was surprised to see them holding hands and mostly at ease with each other, though there was still tension in the air. She smiled softly when she saw me, and I could see how relieved she was that I was okay.

My dad tensed up even more the closer they got. His gaze zeroed in on the vest I was wearing, and his face twisted with anger. "You can't be serious. I'm not going to let another one of my daughters be with a—"

"Watch it," Cash growled, taking a step closer and making the blood drain from my dad's face.

Crossing my arms against my chest, I glared at

him. "You don't get a say in my life anymore. And that has nothing to do with Cash. The only person to blame for that is you."

He sputtered for a second, then his shoulders slumped as he sighed. "I know I messed up, but does that really mean I shouldn't get a say in my daughters' lives anymore?"

"Pretty much," I muttered. " And I'm definitely not going to let the man who hid Mom and me from his wife and daughter for my whole life have a say in who I'm with. "

"She's got a point," my mom said with a shrug. Hurt crept into her eyes, but when she looked at my dad, I could still see how much she loved him. When I thought about my growing feelings for Cash, it was hard not to have some understanding of why she might forgive my dad.

"Fine," he huffed, shooting a glare at Cash. Though I noticed he kept his distance from my man. "But you better take good care of her."

"I'll do a better job of it than you, that's for damn sure," Cash growled.

Before the two could continue their verbal sparring, my mom asked me, "How are you doing, honey?"

I reached out and took her hand, giving it a soft

squeeze before Cash hauled me back against him. "I'm okay, Mom. Cash has helped me deal with a lot of this, and he takes amazing care of me."

She flashed him a small but genuine smile as he dropped onto the couch, then captured my wrist and tugged me down to sit next to him before interlacing our fingers. "Thank you for looking after my daughter."

He accepted her gratitude with a dip of his chin. "My pleasure."

My parents sat on the couch across from us, and I didn't miss how my mom stayed close to my dad and let him hold her hand on his leg.

"Are you two"—I struggled with how to define their relationship, knowing he was married to another woman—"going to stay together?"

"We are," my mom confirmed with a nod. "It won't be easy with the future ahead of us. Your dad has a lot of work to do before he can earn my trust back." She looked at him, and when their eyes met, I knew that no matter what my dad had done, he really did love my mom. "But we're working on it."

I leaned against Cash's side, feeling oddly relieved they were staying together. I was still so angry with my dad, but that didn't mean I'd just stopped loving him. And I wanted my mom to be happy. If that meant being with my dad, then I hoped they could find happiness in the rough road ahead. "Working on it?"

"We had a meeting with the divorce lawyer, and he's going to try to expedite the process so that we can get married before..." She trailed off for a second, her eyes clouding with fear. "In case we have to be apart. Otherwise, we won't have legal rights to any part of his life. And I found him a therapist as well as a marriage counselor for us to see together."

I blinked a few times, surprised by her answer. She'd really thought this through, and I couldn't say I wasn't proud of her for the way she was handling the situation "Wow. That's a lot to cram into the short time since I've seen you."

My dad nodded and let go of my mom's hand to put his arm around her. "I'm lucky your mom will stand by me after everything I've done." There was no missing the love in his eyes as he turned to look at her. "I'll do whatever it takes to make it up to her. And anything I can do to make sure that she's happy and that I'm by her side."

His comment made me wonder about how the court case was proceeding. "Does your attorney think you'll end up in jail?" I asked, cocking my head to the side.

His expression was grave as he nodded. "We met with him as well. Unfortunately, it's almost certain that I won't be able to avoid incarceration. But he's confident that I'll be able to minimize the length of my sentence if I turn state's evidence on the people who bribed me. Especially since prosecuting them could be a huge boost to the career of the state's attorney."

I felt Cash tense next to me. "Any of those people as dirty as Bickle?"

My dad shook his head, quickly assuring him, "No, he was the worst of the lot. And the others don't have organizations to back them. My testimony won't put Karina or Kiara at risk."

"Good," Cash bit out. "'Cause if you put my woman in danger again—"

"I won't," my dad growled adamantly.

"You're really going to testify against all of them?" I asked.

"Absolutely." My dad brushed his fingers across my mom's knuckles. "I meant it when I said I'd do whatever it takes, and that means owning up to my mistakes and dealing with the consequences. And if I can make sure those other crooks pay for their crimes, earning a shorter time away from my family... that's a start. I need to make things right so I don't drag you girls and your mom into my mess any more than I already have."

I would never completely trust my dad again, but his answers and seeming determination gave me hope that maybe one day, we could patch our relationship. And perhaps he could do so with Kiara, too.

I was happy to usher Karina's parents to the door once they'd finished their visit. It seemed like the meeting had been good for her, but it had clearly exhausted her as well. She sagged into my side, so I swept her into my arms and carried her to our room.

When I laid her down on the bed and ordered her to rest, she halfheartedly protested but fell asleep a minute later. Figuring she would rest easier if I held her, I removed her clothes, undressed myself, and climbed into bed. But before I could wrap myself around her, my phone vibrated on the nightstand. Grunting in annoyance, I leaned back and grabbed my cell. It was a text from Mac. *Fuck.*

Mac: My office.

Me: Be there in five.

I pulled the covers up over Karina and carefully scooted off the mattress so I wouldn't wake her. This whole situation caused her too much stress, which wasn't good for her. Especially if my boys had done their job and knocked her up.

After dressing in jeans, boots, a black T-shirt, and my cut, I left a note for Karina telling her to rest. Since her vest hadn't come yet, I ordered her to stay in the room until I returned. Then I headed down to meet with my prez.

Scout, Dax—our sergeant at arms—and a couple of our enforcers were all in the office with Mac when I arrived.

"Waiting on Knight," Scout informed me. I nodded and shuffled over to the wall to lean against it. Knight showed up seconds behind me, and Mac told him to close the door when he walked in.

"My friend in Phoenix has a contact in Bickle's organization," Dax informed us. "He sent a date and time for Bickle's location. He's meeting with a potential drug distributor, so depending on how Cash and Knight want to handle this..." He trailed off because we all understood his meaning.

Mac scratched his beard as he contemplated,

then glanced at me and Knight, who had come to stand next to me. "Take Dax and at least three other brothers with you," he told me. "Handle your business. Quietly and cleanly. We don't want any of the other assholes that Timkins will name to get wind and disappear."

I nodded, and Mac turned to Knight. "Before you head out, take Kiara to the clubhouse. Bridget and a couple of other old ladies will come to keep your women calm and distracted. We'll have more than enough guards on them, so they'll be safe."

"Don't forget to call Dash," Scout added. "Give him a heads-up that you might need a cleaning crew after you take care of Bickle."

"Will do," I said as Knight grunted his own agreement. We discussed a few more details, then I headed out. Just before I exited into the hall, Mac called my name.

"Yeah?" I responded as I pivoted around. He threw a piece of leather at me, and I easily caught it. When I realized what it was, a grin split my face.

"How'd you find one so damn fast?" I asked incredulously.

When the brothers started dropping like flies, falling fast and hard for their women, Mac had ordered a stash of Silver Saints "Property of" vests to keep at the compound. Then all we had to do was send it out to be embroidered, and we had it back in a few days. But Karina didn't have a typical figure, and Mac hadn't had one that would fit around her big, sexy as fuck tits. Kiara had a very similar figure, and they'd given her the only one that worked for their body type.

Mac told me he'd order more, but it would take a couple of weeks and then several days to add her name to the property patch. It had only been two, so I was almost speechless when I held up the leather vest that read, "Property of Cash."

"Called in a favor," he grunted as he stood and gathered up his wallet and keys. "Figured you'd want one on her when you left to deal with Bickle."

"I owe you," I told him.

"Yes, you do," he agreed, his tone completely serious, but a smirk played on his lips. "Go be with your woman. I'm going home to mine."

Karina was still asleep when I returned to our room, and though it wasn't very late, I undressed and joined her in bed.

I didn't sleep. I just held her curvy body and thought about what I would say to her. The meeting was set for the next day in the early evening, and as much as I wanted to shield her from all of this bullshit, she'd had enough people in her life lying and keeping secrets from her.

It was nearly midnight when she stirred and turned her head to look back at me with a sweet, sleepy smile. "Sorry, I didn't mean to sleep the rest of the day away."

I kissed her forehead and tightened my arms around her. "You obviously needed the rest."

"Well, I'm awake now," she murmured, then yawned.

Chuckling, I buried my face in the crook of her shoulder. "Do you need help getting back to sleep, sunshine?" My arm was curved around her waist, and as I asked the question, I glided my palm up to cup one of her heavy, round globes. Then I trailed my lips along her shoulder and grinned when a shiver wracked her body. She moaned, and I gently squeezed her breast while bucking my hips as she pressed her ass back into me.

"Yes," she breathed when my other hand slipped between her legs.

"Yes? You need help going back to sleep?" I crooned as I dragged my middle finger up her slit and circled her clit.

"You," she gasped when I entered her with two digits. "Need you."

"Always, sunshine. You'll always have me," I promised.

By the time she passed out again, I'd worn her out with three orgasms and managed to fill her unprotected womb twice more.

"I won't be long, sunshine." I sat on the couch and bent over to pull on my boots and tie the laces.

"Where are you going?" Her tone surprised me, so I glanced up and almost laughed because she looked so fucking adorable. She tried to look intimidating, but her small stature, curvy body, perfect face, and natural allure made it hard to take her anger seriously.

"Got to go to a meeting," I told her as I finished up with my boots.

We'd awoken slowly that morning, and I devoured her sweet pussy for breakfast. Then I picked her up and took her into the bathroom with me for a shower. When we were done, I had dried us both off and gave her a pat on the ass, telling her to get dressed.

She must have picked up on my tension as I pulled on my clothes because she kept glancing at me curiously. When I mentioned that I had to go out, her eyes had narrowed suspiciously.

Again, I was tempted to lie to her so I could shield her from anything that might cause her pain. But that would put a bigger wedge between us than her simply being angry because I put myself in danger by going to meet with the enemy.

Finished, I stood and picked up my cut from the table and shrugged it on. Then I walked over to the couch and grabbed the vest Mac had given me the night before. She stood beside the bed with her arms crossed and glared at me. I sauntered over and helped her put her arms through the holes and set it on her shoulders.

"You go anywhere outside this room and you wear this, got it?"

Karina's eyes had gone from narrowed to wide and round. "Is this...?"

I took her hand and led her into the bathroom, turning her just enough that she could see the back of the vest in the mirror.

"Property of Cash," she read. Her voice trembled, and I whipped her back around to see what was wrong.

Fuck. It never occurred to me that she wouldn't want to wear my brand. But instead of finding her upset, she beamed at me and threw herself into my arms.

I took her mouth in a deep, possessive kiss, holding her to me with one hand on her juicy ass and the other splayed over the writing that marked her as mine. When things were about to get out of hand, I forced myself to let her go and kissed her forehead.

"I've gotta go, sunshine."

"You found him, didn't you?"

I sighed and nodded. "Crashing a meeting and having a word with the motherfucker."

"I'm going." She stated, as if she really believed I would ever let that happen.

"Not a fucking chance in hell, Karina," I growled. "Your ass is staying right here where I know you'll be safe."

"I want to face the man who ruined my life," she growled right back.

"Sunshine, I love that you're strong, courageous, and independent. But I also know you aren't stupid, and you need to consider what's about to happen without emotion fogging your brain. You think I could concentrate on anything except you if I let you come with me? I need to be focused. This man is deadly. I won't risk losing you or letting you spend your life with some other fucker because I got myself a bullet in the head."

Karina's expression filled with fear, and while I hated to scare her, I needed her to understand the reality of the situation.

"Do this for me, sunshine. Stay here and let me protect you. Besides"—I placed my hand gently on her soft stomach—"I know you'd never endanger our baby."

Karina's mouth formed a little O, then she shook her head and sputtered, "I'm—I'm not--I can't be pregnant!"

I grinned and gave her a quick, hard kiss. "I've been fucking you bare every chance I got, sunshine. I'm willing to bet you're knocked up. But if you're not, I'll just keep trying until I put a baby in your belly."

I took advantage of her shock and kissed her again, then guided her over to the couch and handed her a pair of sneakers. "Kiara will be here any minute. You can hang with the other old ladies and get to know your family while I'm gone."

"Pregnant?"

I laughed at her stunned expression. I wasn't sure she'd heard anything I said after that part of our conversation.

A knock on the door interrupted us, and I shouted for them to enter.

Kiara popped her head in and grinned. "Ready?" she asked Karina. "We've got plans to get into all kinds of trouble and drive our men batshit crazy."

I rolled my eyes and kissed Karina's forehead again before I stood. "Be good," I ordered before walking out the door.

11

KARINA

Staying behind while Cash put himself in danger to clean up the mess my dad had made didn't feel right, but I knew it was what I had to do. I wasn't equipped to face off against a criminal and would only put him in more danger if I didn't stay behind. And if I really was pregnant... I shook off that thought, not ready to think about it. I knew that his club brothers would have his back, but it didn't make the wait any easier.

Luckily, I had my sister and several of the other old ladies to keep me occupied while he was gone. Kiara tugged on my arm and led me over to the bar, nudging me onto a stool before she climbed onto the one to my right. "Have you ever gotten drunk before?"

"No." I shook my head with a soft laugh. "The closest I've ever come was when my mom bought a four-pack of wine coolers for Lorelei and me. As long as we stayed home, she said we could drink them all, so we did. I don't think she expected them to hit us so hard, but we both got buzzed and had horrible hangovers the next morning."

"So you're a lightweight," Cat teased as she set several glasses on the bar top.

"Definitely," I confirmed with a nod.

"Then I guess I'll stick to mimosas for now." She grabbed a bottle of sparkling Moscato and a jug of orange juice from the small fridge behind the bar and started filling the glasses.

"Just juice for me," Kiara murmured.

Cat's head jerked up, and she speared my sister with a knowing look. "You're pregnant?"

"Yeah, it's early days yet, but I took a test, and it was positive." She dropped her hand down to cup her still-flat belly. "I'm kind of surprised Shane has been able to keep the news to himself. He was so excited, but between finding out that I had a sister and all the other drama with my dad, he didn't want me to get overwhelmed."

"Get ready for him to be even more overprotective than usual," Bridget warned.

"Yeah, they regress even further than caveman mode when you're carrying their baby," Arya—Bear's old lady—agreed.

"You're pregnant? I'm going to be an aunt?" I squealed.

Kiara aimed a soft smile my way. "Yeah, Auntie Karina."

"I love the sound of that," I sighed, my heart full to the point that it felt as though it burst.

"I'm so excited to become a mom." Kiara bounced on her stool. "But I also can't wait to be Auntie Kiara. I never thought I'd have that."

My cheeks filled with heat as I thought about how many times Cash had come inside me without any protection. And all of the things he'd said about filling me with his come and knocking me up. What if we got to be pregnant together?

"Just juice for you, too." Cat slid a glass toward me. "To be on the safe side since I recognize that look."

Kiara's eyes widened. "Do you think there's a chance you could also be pregnant?"

"Um...yeah, there's definitely a chance," I whispered, my cheeks getting even hotter.

"Of course, there is." Arya shook her head with a laugh. "The Silver Saints don't waste any time in claiming their women or knocking them up. At the rate we're going, the club won't need to have any outside prospects at some point."

"You're right. We're literally giving birth to the next generation of Silver Saints." Bridget rolled her eyes. "Dane is absolutely going to want to follow in his dad's footsteps."

"Grady, too," Arya agreed.

"And who knows what trouble all the girls are gonna get into." Cat sipped her mimosa.

Bridget took a gulp of hers. "Yeah, Molly and Dahlia are leading the way, that's for sure."

I hadn't met any of the Silver Saints children yet, but I loved how family focused the club seemed to be. I'd always wished for a big family growing up since my mom and I were on our own so often, and now I had a sister and a niece or nephew on the way—and basically a brother-in-law in Knight, even if they weren't married yet. And now it looked like I'd have an even larger extended family with all of the Silver Saint couples and their children.

Any babies Cash and I might have would grow up with so many kids to play with, including cousins. If I was already pregnant...

"We might be pregnancy buddies." Saying it out

loud made the possibility real, and excitement skittered over my nerves. I wanted to have Cash's baby.

"I know." Kiara sniffled. "Is it okay to admit that I really, really hope you're pregnant?"

"More than okay." I reached over and pressed my hand over hers. "I've only known Cash for like a week, but I was thinking the same thing."

"Nobody will judge you for that," my sister reassured me. "I've only been with Shane for a couple of weeks longer."

Bridget shrugged. "And Mac got me pregnant with Molly right after kidnapping me."

"But is it really kidnapping when you provide the ladder?" Cat teased.

"We should ask Oakley sometime since she knows the law better than any of us," Arya suggested.

Bridget nodded. "That girl is going to make a heck of a lawyer when she gets done with all of her schooling. It's a good thing Doc snatched her up because she can use those skills for the club someday."

As they chatted away, my mind was stuck on my possible pregnancy. Instead of freaking out, I found myself looking forward to the possibility. Leaning toward Kiara, I murmured, "It would be amazing for our children to be so close in age. They'd grow up as close as siblings."

"Like we should have been able to do," she muttered. "I'm so mad at Dad for never telling me about you. We missed out on so much time. I don't know how I'll forgive him."

"Neither do I." I heaved a deep sigh and squeezed her hand. "But at least our children won't ever have to go through anything like that. They'll always have each other."

She grinned at me. "Thank goodness Mac sent Cash out to Aspen to get you so you had the chance to fall in love."

"And Grey," I muttered.

"Have you heard anything else from Lorelei?"

I shook my head. "Not yet, but Cash assured me that Grey will take good care of her."

"I'm sure he is." Kiara giggled. "Really, really good care, if you know what I mean."

"Ugh, yeah. I wouldn't be surprised if Lorelei fell for him as hard and fast as I did for Cash." I huffed out a little breath, irritated by the fact that Grey hadn't brought her to the clubhouse like Cash had done with me. I hated not knowing where she was, especially since I felt responsible for her being pulled into this mess in the first place, even though

I'd had no way of knowing that our fun, holiday trip would turn out this way. "I didn't get much of a look at Grey since Cash shoved him into a snowbank when they got to the cabin and then all of my focus was on Cash when they came inside. But even covered in snow, I could tell he was hot."

"Don't ever let Cash hear you say that," Cat advised.

Arya nodded, laughing softly. "Yeah, he might give Grey a black eye to make him less pretty since our men aren't exactly rational when it comes to their women."

"You can say that again." Bridget lifted her glass as though she was making a toast, then finished off her mimosa.

Their banter, easy acceptance of me, and the news of my sister's pregnancy helped loosen some of my tension over what Cash was doing. But not all of it.

When Bridget sidled up next to me to set her glass on the bar top, I asked, "Does it ever get any easier, waiting for the man you love when you know he's in danger?"

"Not really, but you do gain some confidence in the fact that they'll come back to you."

Her answer was about what I expected, but it

wasn't very comforting. "But at least this kind of stuff isn't a regular occurrence, right?"

"I wish I could say stuff like this almost never happens, but then I'd be lying." She patted my back. "Oddly enough, the worst of it usually comes about when one of the guys finds his woman, so I often find myself in the strange position of wondering if I should hope the single guys find someone to love or wish that they don't for a little while so we get a nice break from the turmoil."

"Yeah, I can see the conundrum there." I thought about it for a moment. "But what I feel for Cash is worth anything, so I hope they all find what we have."

Bridget beamed an approving smile at me. "Exactly."

12

We parked our bikes a good mile from the warehouse where we were supposed to find Bickle. On the way out the door, we'd grabbed a couple of prospects to stay behind and watch over our rides.

Scout had decided to come at the last minute to cover our asses from a perch. He'd been a sniper in the military—part of the reason for his road name—and kept his skills in top shape. So he broke off from the group and slinked away to find a spot with the best option.

Knight and I led the way to the warehouse with Dax close behind. Once we reached the compound housing several shipping warehouses, we contacted

Hack, another brother who was one of the best hackers in the world, and he tapped into the security.

"The front gate is open," he said through the Bluetooth earpiece I was wearing. "But there are cameras, and I don't want to tip off the guard watching them by shutting them down. No cameras behind the building."

We crept around, carefully avoiding the barbed wire fencing with big signs stating it was electric. I doubted it was real, and Hack confirmed it a minute later.

"No current, even low grade. It's just for show."

We were all connected so I didn't have to share the information. Instead, I waited for Knight to hop the fence, then followed him over. Dax and Nova were right behind us, then Dom and Breaker.

We split up to check each of the four buildings for signs of activity. Predictably, no cameras were inside them. The seedy deals that happened here couldn't risk being caught on tape.

Knight and I took the first warehouse but didn't find any signs of life. Although the stench made it clear that it was used regularly for things I didn't want to think about.

Nova waved at us when we stepped back

outside. We hurried over and followed him to the third building where our other brothers waited.

"Don't see your mark yet," Dax grunted. "But something is happening."

Breaker's hands fisted, and his knuckles cracked, making his enraged expression all the more intimidating. He lifted his chin toward Nova. "Recognize anyone?"

Nova handed me his phone, and I looked through several pictures he'd taken through a window.

"Fucking hell," I muttered when I saw the leader of a known trafficking ring. He'd been on our radar, but so far, we hadn't infiltrated his organization and taken him down. And he worked for someone bigger, so simply killing him wouldn't disband the organization. Better to take him alive and torture him until he cracked.

"We play this right, we can take care of both," Dom grunted.

Knight's brow furrowed so low I could barely see his eyes. I was sure my expression looked about the same. "I get it, brother," Knight gritted through his clenched jaw. "But Bickle is the mission. We'll find another way to Markoff, but if it comes down to the two, you take out Bickle. Clear?"

I nodded and watched the others contemplate, then lift their chins in agreement one by one.

Dax motioned his head to the right before he and Nova headed around the left side of the building. Breaker and Dom went right, and since there were two back doors, Knight and I each took one.

The security in the place was pathetic. While one of the back doors had a keypad, a simple bolt and cylinder locked the other one. Hack had the electronic one bypassed in seconds, and I picked the lock on the other in almost the same amount of time.

When we realized the first door opened straight into the interior, but mine led to a utility room, Knight joined me, and we entered through there.

We both had every right to be the one to take down that motherfucker Bickle, but we'd agreed that the result, no matter who made the kill, was all that mattered. We wanted to get this done fast and get home to our women.

We waited in the darkness, listening to the activity in the main space while our brothers reported where they'd found a place to wait as well. We were all out of sight, so knowing their locations would make it easier to distinguish each other if the shit hit the fan.

Finally, the front door creaked open, and I

peeked around the corner to see Bickle step inside, flanked by his younger son and several big dudes who looked ready to kill. However, after studying the bodyguards for a minute while they walked over to Markoff, I realized that their expressions were carefully blank, except when Bickle or his son spoke and the guards glanced at each other. There was unspoken communication and a small flash of annoyance whenever their boss spoke.

I tapped Knight's shoulder and jerked my head toward the small group. Knight nodded. "They don't respect or fear him," he concluded under his breath.

"If things get hairy, they're gonna split and leave his ass behind with no protection."

"Scout," Dax murmured over our connection. "Wait for my signal, then fire a warning shot, followed immediately by a non-fatal hit to one of the bodyguards. Make sure the injured one can still turn tail and run."

"Understood," Scout replied.

Bickle, Remus—his son who wasn't in jail—and his men stopped a few feet from Markoff and his crew, who were clearly former Special Forces, and feared their boss enough for us to know that they wouldn't abandon him so easily.

"Come with an explanation?" Markoff asked

Bickle, standing casually with his hands in the pants pockets of his immaculately tailored suit.

Bickle cleared his throat. "The connection we had in the courts got tangled up with the Silver Saints and got himself caught."

Markoff stiffened, but it was barely noticeable unless you studied him closely. "What does he know?"

"Nothing about you," Bickle assured him quickly. "But my other kid was running the operation in Vegas, and since Timkins lost control over his court case, he got the fucking death penalty."

"What about the operation?" Markoff asked, clearly not giving a damn if Bickle lost one of his sons.

"We had to close it down with the cops digging into Joey's life and contacts. But Remus will be taking over, he said, jerking his head toward his son.

"And this is why you haven't delivered more product?"

Bickle swallowed. "We're looking for a new club to lure the girls and changing out the guys who find them, then we'll be up and running again."

What. The. Fuck?

Bickle had been running a trafficking ring in Vegas? From what he was saying, it sounded like if we took him out, the operation would fall apart. But just in case, I'd have a talk with Mac when we got back and send some patches out to investigate and disassemble any remaining remnants of the group.

Mac had a history with the Lennox hotel owner and worked closely with his head of security, Knox, whenever a problem we were handling made its way to Vegas.

Markoff was silent, making Bickle sweat and shuffle his feet, clearly uncomfortable under the scrutiny.

"You have two weeks to get things running and bring me product, or we'll have to have another talk. I have clients with expectations, and if you can't deliver, I'll have to replace you with someone who can."

Every time he called women product, I had to fight the urge to walk in and spray the place with bullets.

"Did he just give us an opening to get someone in there?" Scout mumbled.

"Sounds like it," Hack said.

They went quiet when Markoff spoke again. "You should keep your head down, Bickle," he warned. "My competitors are not happy that you've been collecting on their turf. And if you're not performing, I'll have no reason to protect you. Is that understood?"

"You take out Bickle and Remus without a fuss, and Markoff will think it was an assassination by one of his rivals," Dax muttered.

I knew what he was suggesting, and it was the smart play. But the thought of Bickle not suffering, not dying painfully as he stared into my face and knew he was facing Silver Saints justice...it caused rage to blow through me.

"You expect us to make this clean and simple?" Knight growled. "After he threatened our women?"

Everyone was silent for a minute, then Dax said, "Your call."

Knight and I stared at each other, the need to make Bickle suffer burning in our guts. I wasn't sure I had it in me to do anything except cut Bickle's balls off and feed them to him. Then make him scream some more before he ate a bullet.

But I struggled with the weight of the greater good versus my own need for revenge.

"It's justice either way," Knight finally conceded, though I could tell that he was fighting the same battle.

"It means letting Markoff go," I said, speaking to all my brothers.

No one responded, and I knew it was their way of acknowledging the truth and still leaving the decision in our hands.

Finally, I nodded before I changed my mind.

"Do it," Knight snarled.

It only took a few seconds before Bickle jerked back violently, a hole visible right between his eyes as he fell to the ground when no one attempted to catch him. His son screamed until he met the same fate.

Markoff's men immediately surrounded him, guns drawn and looking all around to find the source of the bullet.

"A warning." Hack's voice came through one of the bodyguard's radios. "Keep your filth out of other people's territories."

Markoff wasn't visible in the circle of his guards, but his voice carried. "What you do now that your boss is dead is up to you."

Bickle's men stared at each other, seemingly unsure of what to do next.

Markoff didn't wait for a response. He and his men moved as a unit to the door and disappeared.

"We don't even have to let them know he's dead," one of the men commented.

Another piped up. "We could run it with him as the fall guy if no one suspects it's us."

Knight suddenly grinned, and I knew he'd had the same thought.

"You want backup?" Nova asked, clearly knowing where our minds had led us.

"Nah," I said.

Knight raised his pistol, and I did the same, then we stalked into the open space, aiming at the heads of the two nearest thugs.

"Gonna have to pass on the promotion, boys," I drawled. "Won't matter anyway because you'll be dead."

The four men had pulled their weapons the second they spotted us, but their actions weren't smooth, and they didn't work as a unit. Knight took a shot at the same time as I did, disarming two with a bullet to the wrist and firing another into the heads of the last two before any of them could get a shot off.

"Just the four of us. Now we're even," Knight drawled.

The two injured men were shaking with rage, and when one bent down to grab his pistol, I shot forward and kicked him in the head, sending him flying backward. After hitting the ground hard, I expected him to stay down, but the idiot struggled to his feet and came rushing at me. "Assholes never fucking learn," I muttered as I stepped to the side and darted around to his back when he lunged for me, taking him off balance. Then I banded an arm around his neck and grabbed his wrist, pressing my thumb directly onto his wound.

He screamed like a little girl and tried to fight free, but I had him in an iron grip.

"We need this one?" I asked.

Knight looked at the other man, who froze and cradled his bleeding hand against his chest. "You gonna play nice?" he queried.

The man nodded and cleared his throat before saying, "Yes. Just don't kill me."

Neither of us answered as I switched my grip so I could break my hostage's wrist. Then when his attention was on his shattered bone, rather than trying to free himself from my hold, I pulled a knife from the holster around my thigh and slit the bastard's throat.

I released him, and he crumpled to the floor. "Don't fucking get up this time," I snarled sarcastically.

He only lasted another minute or so because I'd severed his carotid artery.

The rest of our brothers sauntered in when they saw we had the situation handled.

An hour later, we'd extracted what we could from the guard, and Knight had sliced open the bastard's throat. We let Dash know he needed to get a crew out here to clean the scene, then while the rest of our gang waited for them to arrive, Knight and I took off like bats outta hell, our only thoughts about getting home to our women.

We stopped at Knight's place to clean up the blood and spattered remnants of brain and whatever else was clinging to us. We didn't want to scare the fuck out of Kiara and Karina, but more than that, we didn't want them tainted by the realities of club business. They accepted us for who we were, but that didn't mean we wouldn't do everything in our power to keep them from the seedier parts of our life.

Finally, we headed to the clubhouse, and I felt lighter than I had in years. Karina was the sunshine in my dark life, and nothing would ever come before her.

The minute Cash walked through the door, I raced over and threw myself into his waiting arms. "I was so worried about you."

His hands slid down my back to grip my butt, and he gave one cheek a light slap that only stung a little. "I told you that I had everything under control."

"I know, but I still couldn't help being afraid that something would go wrong."

"I wasn't gonna do anything that would put me at risk now that I found you." He dipped his head to brush his lips against mine. "Love you too much to ever leave you."

Whoa.

Cash loved me.

He'd protected me and taken care of the threat, and I'd always felt safe with him. Knowing that he loved me, though...it filled me with wonder and excitement. Made me feel whole again after all I'd been through.

"I love you, too," I told him with a smile.

"Damn fucking straight, you do," he grunted. I loved how gruff he was on the outside. And that I was the only one who knew how sweet he was on the inside.

After our declarations, I wanted to feel closer to him, so I closed the space between us. He immediately enveloped me in his arms. He was so attentive, always taking care of me. Even in bed, he was always making sure that I got what I needed.

Suddenly, I had the urge to take care of him for a change. To give him something else that I'd never given anyone else. And to show my appreciation for everything he'd given me.

Tugging on his vest, I murmured, "Come upstairs with me. I need to have you all to myself."

"Every part of me belongs to you. I'll follow you anywhere, sunshine."

Butterflies swirled in my belly as we crossed over to the stairs and made our way up to his room. When the door shut behind us, I pulled on his arm so he'd stay where he was instead of heading over to the bed. Then I dropped to my knees and swiftly pulled his belt through the loops before dropping it on the ground.

But he stopped me, putting his large hands over mine. "Sunshine, what do you think you're doing?"

"I want to show you how much you mean to me. How thankful I am," I explained, running my fingers along the seam of his jeans.

His cock was already rock hard behind his zipper. Waiting and ready for me.

But Cash shook his head. "You don't need to do any of that. I love you. Nothing I've done for you was with the thought of getting something back."

"I know, but I want to. I've never had a man in my mouth," I said, looking up at him through my lashes.

"Not gonna turn down that offer when I want all of your firsts, and I've fantasized about having your lips wrapped around me."

He was already pulling his pants down, his cock staring me in the face, and a drip of precome had formed at the tip. I darted my tongue forward, licking it off, and the salty-sweet taste hit the back of my throat.

"Sunshine, that tongue is gonna kill me," he growled.

"Yeah. Do you like that? Want me to keep licking this big dick?" I smiled, looking up to see his eyes at half mast.

He bucked his hips forward. "Yeah. Lick it like it's your favorite popsicle. All the way to the root."

My tongue trailed the long vein leading from his tip all the way down the length of his cock and back up again.

"Like this?" I murmured.

"Yeah, but do that while my cock fills your mouth."

"Oh."

I remember thinking how big his dick was when I first saw it and whether it would ever fit inside my pussy, let alone my mouth. But as I wrapped my lips around his head, I knew we were made to fit together.

He was what I'd been waiting for my whole life.

Who I wanted to be my first everything.

I might not have been the best at my first blow job, fumbling with my hands and trying not to bite his sensitive flesh. I thought I did something wrong when he grabbed the back of my head and yanked me back so I met his beautiful gaze, but the heat in his dark eyes let me know he was enjoying this as much as I was, and his growled words confirmed it. "That feels amazing, but I'm not going to waste my come in your mouth. I need it inside that perfect pussy of yours."

He didn't need to say anything else. I wanted that, too. I'd never thought about kids or the future before I met Cash, but seeing the other women around the club, I wanted to be like them.

To have these men tied to them. Worshipping them. And their babies.

I was going to let him fill me up again. If I wasn't pregnant yet, I wanted to be. Soon.

Cash's shirt was already off before I stripped off my own and then shimmied out of the rest of my clothes. He kissed me deeply, his fingers tangling in my hair as he walked me backward toward the bed.

I was needy and wanted him. Knowing he'd been in danger because of me had heightened my desire to an almost unbearable state. Arching my back up so my pussy brushed against his wet cock, I moaned.

"That's my greedy little pussy," he murmured as his lips trailed down to my neck.

His fingers slipped down my stomach before cupping my sex.

I whimpered, bucking my hips forward, needing

him to do more. To touch me harder. To push me over the edge I was already nearing.

"Such a greedy little pussy, sunshine," he growled before plunging his fingers into my wetness.

"Yes," I breathed, capturing his lips again with my own before riding his fingers.

My body ached for release, and once his thumb found my sensitive nub, I cried out, rocking away my orgasm on his fingers.

I mewled when he pulled his hand away. Staring up at him as he licked my wetness from his skin. "You taste so fucking good. Wanna see for yourself?"

"Mmm-hmm." I darted my tongue forward, licking what was left of my juices off his fingers.

"Oh fuck, sunshine, that's so hot," he growled before his lips were back on mine.

Our tongues mingled as we fell back on the mattress, his arms holding him up, but his hips firmly pressed to mine as I ground against him, feeling the friction of his cock against me. But not right where I wanted it.

"I need you in me," I whimpered, lifting my legs so they wrapped around his waist.

"That's my greedy girl. I'm going to give it to you."

He sat back, pressing his hands into the mattress

on either side of me before plunging his cock deep inside me.

"Feels so good," I moaned, instinctively rocking against him.

"Yeah, take my cock, sunshine." He dipped his head to nip my bottom lip, the slight sting sending a zing of sensation straight to my core. "It feels so good inside you because you're mine. Aren't you?"

"Yes, I'm yours. Only yours," I moaned as a fire started low in my stomach.

My orgasm was building, and it was as if Cash could read my body better than I could. His hand went to my clit, rubbing the sensitive nub as he thrust harder in me. My body quaked as I screamed out, riding the wave of my release.

"You're so fucking beautiful when you come."

"Then make me do it again, Cash," I whimpered, jutting my hips forward.

"Gladly, sunshine." He picked up the pace, rocking his body harder against mine. His fingers stayed on my clit, flicking it in the same motion he moved his dick.

"Tighten that pussy around me. Let me feel that come on my cock. I'm not gonna last much longer," he growled.

My body erupted as I shook around him, a never-

ending orgasm wracking my body. My lids drifted
shut, and I tilted my head back on the pillow as my
body hummed in ecstasy.

"Open your eyes," he commanded.

My gaze rested on his as he lifted my legs high on
his hips. "You're going to watch me while I come.
While I fill you up with my seed, and then I'm going
to push it inside you. Make sure you're good and full
of me."

The heat of his words had my already sizzling
body singing.

I gripped his sides and held on as we both shuddered, our groans in perfect harmony as I felt him
spill into me.

But instead of collapsing on my chest, he kept
pushing his cock, rocking it against me over and over
again.

"Gotta push my come inside you. Don't want to
spill a drop. Make sure you're mine."

"I'll always be yours, Cash."

"Always, sunshine," he repeated. "Same way as
I'm yours."

That was good because I wouldn't have it any
other way.

EPILOGUE

CASH

"You know, you aren't the only one who made this baby," Karina grumbled when I strutted through the clubhouse like a cat who'd gotten the cream. Which I had, many times.

I laughed and stopped to draw her into my arms. "I gotta take credit for something since you're the superhero who has to carry our baby and give birth."

Her lips curved up as I conceded her point. She melted like butter, the way she always did whenever I said sweet things.

"So?" She turned when she heard Kiara's voice and saw her jump up from the couch to run over to us. "Are you?" she asked, practically jumping up and down with excitement.

"Pretty sure the answer is yes," Knight drawled as he took in my puffed-up chest and smug expression. Neither of which I could seem to get rid of.

"Fuck yes, I knocked up my woman," I crowed.

Karina sighed and pinched my arm so I would loosen my hold and she could wiggle out of my embrace. I frowned but didn't pull her back because she immediately hugged her sister.

"I can't believe we get to do this together!" Kiara squealed, jumping up and down again.

"Relax, baby," Knight said as he tugged her into the circle of his arms, leaving me free to glue Karina to my side again. "All that jumping can't be good for you or the baby."

Kiara rolled her eyes. "The baby is basically the size of a pea."

"Don't say pea!" Karina whined as she broke out of my embrace to run to the nearest bathroom.

"Oops," Kiara mumbled, clearly confused.

"Don't worry about it," I assured her with a wave of my hand. "The baby might be the size of a pea right now, but so is her bladder. Karina's been dashing to the bathroom constantly."

"That will pass," Arya said as she wandered over to us. "At least she isn't throwing up every—"

Karina emptying her stomach in the bathroom cut her off, and I raced over, breaking the door in my haste to get in.

"Shit, sunshine, are you okay?" I asked worriedly as I dropped to the ground and held her hair back while she heaved again.

"Guess I spoke too soon," Arya said sympathetically from the doorway.

"Karina?" Kiara popped into sight as well. "Are you ok—" Then she slapped her hand over her mouth, spun around, and darted away with Knight right on her heels.

"We are never having sex again," Karina mumbled after her third round of throwing up, though by this point her stomach was empty.

I might have been worried, but we both knew my woman couldn't fall asleep without me eating her pussy most nights. Since I didn't want to upset her further, I refrained from reminding her of that.

———————

"We are never having sex again!" Karina screamed again—something she'd been threatening ever since she reached ten centimeters—as she bore down, giving one last push before a baby's cry filled the room.

"It's a boy," the doctor announced as she held up our son for us to see. A nurse hurried over and took him to a little station to clean him up and check his vitals. "You did amazing, Karina," Dr. Howard told her with a beaming smile. "I'll be back to check on you in an hour or so."

Just as she left, the nurse appeared at Karina's side and set our squirming infant in his mother's arms. "Damn," I breathed, in awe of my wife and the miracle she'd brought into the world.

"He's perfect," she whispered, her voice clogged with emotion.

"Both of you are perfect," I told her softly. "I don't know how I got so fucking lucky."

"You can't say stuff like that now," Karina admonished with a motherly scowl.

"So you don't want me to tell you how hard it got me just thinking about you carrying our baby? And that I can't wait to fuck another one into your gorgeous body?"

Karina swallowed and shifted on the bed. "We're never having sex again, remember?" she huffed, although it was said with a lot less conviction this time.

I held back a laugh because I didn't want to hurt her feelings. But I doubted I'd be able to wait long before I talked her into letting me fill her unprotected pussy with my come. She was too fucking irresistible, and fuck...seeing her pregnant had been hot as hell.

"WE ARE NEVER HAVING SEX AGAIN!" Karina groaned as she flopped back into my arms, exhausted from the morning sickness that had been hitting her hard for the past week.

"I think our track record would say otherwise," I teased her as I cradled her in my arms and stood. Our need for each other had only grown in the time we'd been together. And even though I'd agreed to wait two years for another baby, there'd been a few...accidents. Now our babies would be born barely a year apart.

Karina sighed as I set her on the sink and readied her toothbrush before handing it to her. "This time, I mean it."

"Okay," I agreed, placating her. Especially since we'd learned when she was pregnant with Callum that Karina's hormones went into overdrive. She'd been horny all the time, and I was more than happy to fulfill her needs.

"Stop being so smug about it," she mumbled after she spit in the sink and rinsed her mouth.

"Not smug, baby. Proud of my family, happier than I ever thought I could be, more in love with you every fucking day...if that makes me look smug"—I shrugged, making her giggle—"then get used to it."

"You always say the sweetest things," she said with a sniffle.

"Don't cry," I ordered. I fucking hated it when she cried. To stop her tears, I added, "Don't forget the rule if you spread that shit around."

Karina's cheeks turned pink, which I thought was adorable, considering how long we'd been together and all the things we'd done to each other.

She hopped down from the sink and sashayed into the bedroom. I followed her and watched curiously as she picked up her phone from the desk. "What are you up to, sunshine?"

"Just calling Kiara to tell her how sweet my man is."

"You angling for a spanking, sunshine?"

She batted her eyelashes and raised the phone to her ear.

"Thought we were never having sex again?" I drawled, trying not to laugh.

Karina sighed and tossed her phone onto the couch. "You won't always win," she huffed as she started removing her clothes.

"Sunshine, as long as I have you and our family, I've already won everything."

EPILOGUE

KARINA

My dream of having a big family had come to fruition. My babies growing up with an awesome dad who was there for every milestone, an aunt and uncle who loved them almost as much as we did, cousins who were like siblings, and an entire club that was family.

They also had a grandmother and grandfather who lived to spoil them. My dad's criminal case progressed quickly, and he was only sentenced to fourteen months of jail time. With parole, he was back home in just under a year, so he hadn't missed much after Kaylee—Kiara and Knight's first—and Callum were born.

Being in prison had changed him. Even before I managed to mostly forgive him for everything he'd done, he still reached out several times a week after his release just to let me know that he was thinking about Callum and me. And as the kids got older—and multiplied—he showed up for all their activities. Even all their toddler classes, like toddler tumbling and mini music. He showed up for them in ways he'd never been able to with me, and I appreciated it.

There were some exceptions, though. My parents weren't at the compound today for the big barbecue since my dad didn't spend much time around the club. After what he'd almost done to Rom —and how much his secrets had hurt Kiara and me— he'd only ever received a lukewarm welcome when he came around. Not that he ever complained. He knew that he'd earned their mistrust.

Crosby came toddling over and pulled me out of my thoughts. Crouching low, I sighed over the chocolate stain on his T-shirt. "Did someone let you into the brownies already, baby boy?"

"Nuh-uh." He shook his head. "Ice cream!"

"I should've known." My middle child had been hooked on ice cream ever since his daddy gave him his first taste when he turned one. He would happily eat it for every meal if only we'd let him. "Did you have a hot dog first?"

The way his eyes widened as he nodded let me

know he probably hadn't finished it, which my husband confirmed as he walked over to us with our daughter Camila strapped to his chest and a plate with slices of uneaten hot dog in his hand.

Stabbing one of the pieces with a fork, I held it next to his lips. "If you eat all five pieces, you can have another small scoop of ice cream later."

"Yay!" he cheered, opening his mouth wide so I could feed him before doing a little dance.

I beamed a smile at Cash. "Thanks for making sure he got one without grill marks on it."

"He would've screamed the yard down if I dared to serve him a striped hot dog." Cradling the back of Camila's head with his free hand, he leaned over to brush his lips against mine. "Crosby has no problem making sure everyone within a mile radius knows if he's unhappy about something."

I laughed as I fed our toddler another bite. "Probably because he's always trying to get his big brother's attention."

Callum was only a year older—close enough in age to Kiara's middle child that we got to experience most of our second pregnancies together too—and he was Crosby's favorite person in the world. Callum was a mama's boy, Camila was a daddy's girl, but Crosby was a big brother's boy all the way.

"Very true," Cash agreed, his gaze darting over to the bouncy house where our eldest son was currently playing. "The only reason he didn't kick up a fuss about eating a hot dog in the first place was because Callum scarfed one down first."

"Thank goodness one of our sons is a good eater." I heaved a deep sigh and stroked my finger across Camila's chubby cheek. "This one, too."

"At least none of yours are as picky as Kennedy," Kiara complained as she joined us. "I swear, she and Crosby come up with a whole new list of foods they hate every time they're together, and then she adds a dozen more when she gets home. Including things that she loved the day before."

"She's definitely a handful."

"That's for sure," she muttered.

Crosby asked for a drink, so Cash gave me a quick kiss before he led him over to one of the picnic tables to get him one.

"My mom mentioned that Kennedy loved the ground beef and rice casserole she made when the kids were all over at their house last week. I'm sure she'd be happy to give you the recipe. Maybe it hasn't been added to the no-go list yet," I suggested.

"I just might do that," she murmured.

"I'm glad." I darted a glance at her and decided

to broach a subject I'd been avoiding for years. "Sometimes I feel bad bringing up my mom and our dad since they worked through all of their problems and are so happy together now."

Kiara waved off my concern. "You shouldn't. That water is well under the bridge. My mom never made him happy and is already on her third rich husband, for goodness' sake."

Remembering how awful she'd said the last wedding was, I cringed. "Did she invite you to this one?"

"Nope." She shook her head and laughed. "She wasn't a fan of how I turned her down last time. Now I'm just another skeleton in her closet that she doesn't want exposed to whatever man she's managed to hoodwink long enough to get the ring on her finger. You won the mom lottery compared to me."

"I'm more than happy to share mine with you."

Kiara beamed a smile at me. "You'd better. Most of what I've learned about being a good mom has come from watching her."

"You're an awesome mom."

"So are you."

Yeah, I'd definitely found the perfect family.

Want another read with some action while you're waiting for our next Silver Saint release? Check out the Black Ops Series!

If you sign up for our newsletter, you'll get an email from us with a link to claim a free copy of The Virgin's Guardian, which is no longer available to purchase.

And if you're on Facebook, join us in Fiona's Smutaholics!

ABOUT THE AUTHOR

The writing duo of Elle Christensen and Rochelle Paige team up under the Fiona Davenport pen name to bring you sexy, insta-love stories filled with alpha males. If you want a quick & dirty read with a guaranteed happily ever after, then give Fiona Davenport a try!

Don't miss out on new release news and giveaways; sign up for our newsletter!

Printed in Dunstable, United Kingdom